Praise for *No Stars i.*

"*No Stars in the Sky* offers wonderful, haunting writing that burrows deep into the reader's heart. In these stories, Latin American women scramble with courage and stamina to persevere in the face of violence, illegal incarceration, abandonment, migration, solitude, and ruptured relationships. Bátiz's prose is raw, honest, and immediate. To appreciate its beauty, one has only to take in the opening sentence to the story 'Uncle Ko's One Thousand Lives': 'When no one expected his return anymore, when almost everyone believed he must be dead, he appeared out of nowhere at our door.'"

— Lawrence Hill, author of *The Book of Negroes, The Illegal,*
and *Beatrice and Croc Harry*

"Profoundly moving and beautifully written, Martha Bátiz's *No Stars in the Sky* spans different countries and timelines but always circles back to keen observances of the human experience. With a writing style so gorgeous and spare, Bátiz has a remarkable capacity to draw out moments both significant and small, to find the deepest meaning in little snippets of time. Each story is its own universe that transports the reader through the characters' joy and pain, turmoil and resilience, from the hills of inland Mexico to the streetcars of Toronto and beyond. A brilliant collection."

— Amy Stuart, author of *Still Mine, Still Water, and Still Here*

"These are stories for the twenty-first century. Their geography is as vast as their violence. Bátiz has a powerful gift for empathy, entering the mind of a disappeared boy in Argentina, a fourteen-year-old girl exploited at the US/Mexico border, and female asylum seekers sharing

their grief. The power of these stories comes from the writer's understanding of the politics of exploitation and her refusal to look away."

— Rosemary Sullivan, author of *Stalin's Daughter*
and *The Betrayal of Anne Frank*

"*No Stars in the Sky* is a beautifully written, masterfully crafted collection that explores the trauma of loss. Its vivid characters stayed with
me long after I finished the book."

— Marina Nemat, author of *Prisoner of Tehran*
and *After Tehran*

"Brimming with unforgettable characters who find themselves in
unimaginable circumstances *No Stars in the Sky* shines with brilliance
and will leave you breathless. Bátiz's prose sparkles against the dark
background of heartbreaking choices and harsh realities, and lights
up the senses. This book is meant to be read slowly and savoured."

— Christina Kilbourne, author of *Safe Harbour*
and *The Limitless Sky*

"In *No Stars in the Sky*, Martha Bátiz travels across countries and
cultures with confidence, humour, and an ear for the musicality of
language. Her stories, both beautiful and terrifying, deal with loss,
depression, injustice, and the need to love and be loved. A refreshing
collection written by an author in full control of her literary style."

— Pura López-Colomé, author of *Speaking in Song*
and *Borrosa Imago Mundi*

No Stars in the Sky

stories

MARTHA BÁTIZ

ASTORIA

Published in Canada in 2022 and the USA in 2022 by House of Anansi Press Inc.
www.houseofanansi.com

House of Anansi Press is committed to protecting our natural environment.
This book is made of material from well-managed FSC®-certified forests, recycled
materials, and other controlled sources.

House of Anansi Press is a Global Certified Accessible™ (GCA by Benetech)
publisher. The ebook version of this book meets stringent accessibility standards
and is available to students and readers with print disabilities.

26 25 24 23 22   1 2 3 4 5

Library and Archives Canada Cataloguing in Publication

Title: No stars in the sky : stories / Martha Bátiz.
Names: Bátiz Zuk, Martha Beatriz, author.
Identifiers: Canadiana (print) 20220132887 | Canadiana (ebook) 20220132925 |
ISBN 9781487010027 (softcover) | ISBN 9781487010034 (EPUB)
Classification: LCC PS8603.A865 N6 2022 | DDC C813/.6—dc23

Book design: Lucia Kim

*House of Anansi Press respectfully acknowledges that the land on which we operate is the
Traditional Territory of many Nations, including the Anishinabeg, the Wendat, and the
Haudenosaunee. It is also the Treaty Lands of the Mississaugas of the Credit.*

With the participation of the Government of Canada
Avec la participation du gouvernement du Canada

*We acknowledge for their financial support of our publishing program the Canada Council
for the Arts, the Ontario Arts Council, and the Government of Canada.*

Printed and bound in Canada

MIX
Paper from
responsible sources
FSC® C103567

For Edgar, Ivana, Natalia, and Marco: the loves of my life.
For my Fairy Godmother, Dr. Gillian Bartlett.

Dear Reader:

These stories, like so many stories in the world, were born out of personal pain. They are also a way of expressing my sadness and outrage at certain political and social injustices taking place around us, particularly in Latin America. The details in these stories are fictional but reflect disturbing realities. Make no mistake: these realities disturb me, too. Pain that goes unspoken and unseen cannot ever heal, so it is important to face it, to confront it, no matter how hard that may be. That is precisely why I worked so hard to turn the stories that comprise *No Stars in the Sky* into an accurate reflection of our time. It would have been dishonest of me to sugar-coat certain situations to make them more palatable. If you are triggered by violence against women, suicide, racism, injustice, and loss, perhaps it would be wise for you to sit this book out. But if you are ready to catch a glimpse of strong characters making the best of their lives against all odds, it will be my honour to guide you on a journey that, I hope, will leave you forever changed.

Muchas gracias,

Martha Bátiz
Toronto, 2022

Contents

Jason

"YOU CAN'T STAY there forever," Ben says, trying to muffle his desperation.

Ben is losing his patience. He looks so much like Jason right now. Or rather, Jason looked like him. Same pointy nose and ears, almost elfin, and the same blue eyes. I touch the wall. *Blue Lagoon 2054-40*—a colour I chose after many visits to the hardware store comparing samples. I wanted to sleep engulfed in the balminess of those blue eyes. I wanted that blue to watch me, to touch me, to be with me. I close my hand into a fist and punch the wall. It hurts. I discover a bit of paint missing around an old nail and scratch at it, revealing the white drywall beneath. My index finger bleeds a little and I enjoy it. I want to peel off the paint, to peel off my skin.

Ben breathes through his teeth, loudly, and leaves. I am relieved and as I peel tiny lagoons of paint off the wall,

I remember Jason talking about crabs. How they outgrow their shells and shed them.

"It's called molting," he'd said, and I wish I had video-taped him saying it so I could hear his eight-year-old voice again. Molting. It can take months, sometimes. How long will it take me to peel the paint from the entire bedroom?

BEN WAS RIGHT: I cannot stay in bed forever. I must use the washroom. A stranger gazes back at me when I look into the mirror. My eyebrows have gone grey, yet I got my period this morning. What a joke, I think, to have my body remind me at this precise moment that I am empty inside. I inspect my greasy hair, my swollen eyes. The few hairs that grow on my chin have decided not to match my eyebrows and are still black and coarse. I wish my entire body were covered in hair, like thorns. Perhaps it would make me stronger.

The red stains on my underwear take me back to the days when I used to lie on medical tables, feet in the stirrups, my body a war zone where injections, bloodletting, ultrasounds, medications, prayers, and sperm failed to create the miracle of life. Ben masturbating in the room next door, looking at naked women (and men?) who were nothing like us, while I lay open-legged in front of yet another doctor who promised us success. And then, when we were about to give up, a faint hormone count, a linea nigra writing a promise from my pubic bone to my belly button, my breasts full of hope and milk, and Jason, finally, after nine long months, in my arms. I suppress the urge to open the photo albums and inspect our pictures. I know my favourites by heart: the one where Ben is hugging me from behind, cradling my pregnant belly; the one where we're together, crying with joy, holding our newborn baby; the one where you can clearly tell, for the first time, that Jason will have his father's deep blue eyes.

My arms hurt. Their emptiness hurts. So do the bruises. I've been wearing long sleeves, so Ben doesn't notice that I've been pinching my arms—pinching them out of hatred, because there is now nothing for them to hold.

I GO BACK to bed and look up at the ceiling. I regret having paid extra for the smooth finish. A textured ceiling would be more interesting to look at. The room at my mother's house when I was growing up had what is called a popcorn finish. I can picture it perfectly because, after my first boyfriend broke up with me, I spent three weeks in bed, crying, listening to Edith Piaf records, and wondering what had gone wrong and how would I manage to continue living. Everything hurts so much when you're sixteen. Everything seems so hopeless. I remember driving my father's car at full speed thinking I wanted to crash.

I remember wanting to walk into traffic at a busy intersection. What stopped me? And why didn't it stop him?

"HOW WAS SCHOOL?" I asked, serving Jason a spoonful of mashed potatoes, his favourite.

"Fine, but I'm not hungry," he replied, leaving the plate untouched.

I should have known something was wrong then. I should have insisted that he eat. But I had been sixteen once and self-conscious about my weight, so I tried to be understanding. He was a straight-A student, popular among his friends. Why worry? Ben was happy to eat whatever our son didn't want — "Dad's like that little dinosaur under the Flintstones's kitchen sink that eats everything," Jason used to say — so I let it be. Then he stopped showering. He started skipping classes. His grades dropped.

"Where were you? The principal called," I'd scolded him. But instead of answering, he rushed up to his bedroom and slammed the door behind him. Why hadn't I run after him to demand an answer? I did, once, and he pushed me so hard I almost fell down the stairs. We didn't tell Ben. Jason apologized, looked genuinely frightened. We were both afraid.

I clench my teeth now at the memory. My eyes well up, and by the time Ben comes into the room I am curled up in a corner of the bed.

"Let's get you in the shower, babe. Come on," he says, gently. I curl up even tighter, pretending to be a millipede. Jason would have been able to read my body. He was the one who taught me about millipedes to begin with. I want to be one, but Ben won't let me. He pulls the bedsheets away and I let out a whimper.

"You smell bad. I'll get the bed clean for you," Ben says, his blue eyes fixed on mine. Only then do I notice his hair has gone grey, too. He reminds me of his father. He's holding the stained blanket in his hand. "I need to wash this."

I bring my nose to my armpit, then lift the T-shirt to my nose and inhale. A knot curls up in my throat.

"It doesn't smell like him anymore, Ben!"

He drops the blanket and sits down beside me, possibly trying to decide whether to hug me or not. I cry harder.

"I'll bring you another shirt from his drawer," he says.

But I don't want that. I want one from his laundry hamper. I want one that smells like him. Like his teenage deodorant and cologne and sweat. Only his dirty clothes hold traces of his life. I want to wear him.

Ben holds up a tissue for me and I blow my nose. I dry my eyes. He leads me to the washroom and turns on the shower. I let him undress me, forgetting about the bruises on my arms.

"What happened here? What have you been doing to yourself?" he asks, looking at me with pity and concern. I don't know how to answer, so I hug the T-shirt I've been wearing for days until the water is warm enough for me to get in. Ben applies shampoo to my hair, washes my body with soap.

I remember how I used to wash Jason's body when he was little. It was always a struggle to get him into the water because he'd rather keep playing with his toys or watching TV.

"Jason! Bath time!" I would call from upstairs.

His usual reply of "Not yet!" was almost a ritual, repeating itself until I lost my patience and went downstairs to fetch him.

"I'm a T-Rex and I'm going to get you!" I roared.

Jason would laugh and correct me: "You're more like a diplodocus, Mom. But good try!"

I'd pretend to get angry and we'd both go upstairs, laughing. Then he would get in the water and enjoy the touch of my hands as I rubbed his back and lathered his scalp. I loved the aroma of his freshly washed hair, the lotion I applied to his body. I make a mental note to buy more of it so I can inhale and think of him.

THE SILENCE IN the bathroom brings me back to the present. I wonder what Ben's thinking about. I know not to ask because he always gives me the strangest answers. Like that time after dinner, when I asked him what he was thinking about and he said, "The Romans." Who thinks about the Romans? I'm about to ask if he remembers how much Jason enjoyed the loofah when he tells me to take my time rinsing while he changes the bedsheets. He leaves before I can ask any questions. I panic—which bedsheets? Jason's? But I need those. I'll sleep better if I can curl up against the shape of his body. I rush out of the shower to tell Ben I want to sleep in Jason's room, but I slip and fall, making everything wet around me.

"Where are you going?" Ben asks, exasperated. "Why couldn't you wait?"

"The bedsheets! I want Jason's bedsheets." I mumble, ashamed.

Ben looks at me, annoyed, concerned.

"The ones that were on his bed?"

I nod.

"Don't you remember?"

I shake my head. Remember what?

"You buried him in them. You wanted his coffin to have his bedsheets and his blanket. You wanted him to—"

I feel my eyes opening wide.

"To be more comfortable," I say, my voice cracking at the memory of Jason's empty bed. I remember asking the lady at the funeral home to make sure he was covered, to keep him warm. My son never liked the cold, I told her. He was scared of the dark.

"Come on, get up. Are you hurt?" Ben helps me to my feet. "Careful with the puddle on the floor," he adds, as if water could hurt me, as if there was anything else in the world that could hurt me.

I AM BACK in bed, looking at the dismal, featureless ceiling. I wish it were a movie screen where I could replay our happiest moments with Jason. His first birthday. The unexpected instant he touched the sand at the beach and raised his foot up saying, "Ew! Gross!" The moment he learned to ride a bike. When he bit into a hot dog and lost his first tooth. All those times he talked about spiders and crocodiles. The nights he came to our bed, right here, and cuddled up between us, hiding from nightmares. He came to us to feel safe, but I was the one who was comforted by his little foot beside me, the smell of strawberry toothpaste on his breath, the soft rhythm of his beating heart.

I remember all of these things. The morning routine: get up, get dressed, have breakfast, make lunch, kiss goodbye, go to school, go to work, come back from work and school, have dinner together, talk about our days, do homework, take a shower, read a story, go to sleep. Repeat. If only life were a video where you could hit the rewind button. I would press that button endlessly, to experience that precious routine again and again.

I lift the T-shirt I'm wearing to my nose and inhale. Yes, it smells like him. Only it's the him that wouldn't talk anymore. The him who didn't want to share any details about his life with me. The him who wasn't really him anymore. Ben had said it would pass, that it was just a phase.

"He's a teenager," he said.

Ben walks into the room carrying a tray of food and I'm suddenly furious because it wasn't a phase, and it didn't pass. And how was "he's a teenager" supposed to help anyone? The moment he's close enough, I knock the tray up in the air and cry, "I hate you, I hate you, I hate you!" until my yelling becomes sobbing and then nothing because I'm drowning in my voice and my tears.

I'm alone in the room and there are broken plates on the floor and food all over the clean bedsheets. I realize the soup was hot and my skin is burning, my leg is blistering, but I don't care because my shirt no longer smells like him but like tomato sauce, and the red stain will never wash away, yet his smell will.

I wish I were a praying mantis, but I remember Jason was afraid of them because the mommies eat the daddies, and I hate Ben even more.

THE CHURCH WAS full, standing room only. Jason hated going to church and I told Ben we should hold the service elsewhere, but he wouldn't hear of it. I don't remember what was said, which passages of the Bible were read. I don't recall who was there, only that many young people came over to me with stories I had never heard, stories about hilarious things that Jason had done. Young people I had never met who said they were close friends of his. I tried to listen but it was too much, too much. The church was full and some people weren't wearing black. I felt like telling them off—how dare you show up not wearing black, don't you know that my son is dead? But I wasn't strong enough. Ben had to hold me up by the arm, and it took a huge effort for me to stay composed. I had just kissed my dead son's cheeks. He was cold—it took me by surprise and I shivered. Stupid! What was I expecting? That coldness was all I could think about when Mass began. My attention was focused on my lips and the indelible memory they now held. I wanted to scream. There is my son, I thought, staring at his casket. He will remain there forever. His body will swell and decompose in that box. My beautiful son's blue eyes will be pushed out of their sockets, his inner organs will explode, and his rosy skin will turn black before he's reduced to mere bones. He was once an unborn child kicking vigorously inside my womb. It had been a miracle to feel such movement. But now, nothing. Soon to be dust.

• • •

BEN COMES IN, mop and bucket in hand, to clean up my mess. I'm ashamed of myself and get out of bed to help. My leg hurts because of the burn, but I say nothing. Together, we pick up pieces of ceramic and bits of food, in silence. I help him change the bedsheets again and reluctantly agree to change into another one of Jason's T-shirts.

"Thank you for helping," Ben says, his blue-lagoon eyes fixed on mine. They have lost their spark but they are still beautiful. Jason's eyes. I stare at Ben, trying to find my son.

"DO YOU KNOW where Jason is?" I asked Ben over the phone, flustered, in a hurry, on the way to my car. "They called from school. He didn't show up again, they're worried. I've been calling him on his cell phone and at home but there's no answer."

"Again? Tell him he's really in trouble this time!" Ben blurted out.

I hung up. I had to find him. I drove too fast, running red lights and coasting through stop signs, trying to get back to the house as quickly as possible. Everything felt wrong.

When I got home, I ran up the stairs to Jason's room, searching for the right words to say. I wanted to see him. Now I can't un-see him, un-find him, un-live my scream, my attempt to revive him only to discover how heavy he was, how open his eyes were, so open and blue and lifeless.

There had been an empty pill container—where did he get that? The ambulance, the police car; Ben's face, his eyes a tempestuous ocean. He hugged me but I hit him. I hit him on the chest, yelling, "I told you! I told you!"

"MOMMY, WHAT DO you think I should be when I grow up?" Jason asked me once when we were in the car. I looked in the rear-view mirror and found his face.

"I don't know, honey. Whatever makes you happy."

He looked very serious then, and I took advantage of being stopped at a red light to admire his face. He was growing so fast! Almost ten in a couple of months.

"I think I want to be a mathematician like Daddy, and an administrator like you, but also a scientist who works with insects and dinosaurs."

I laughed.

"That sounds perfect, my love."

It was supposed to be perfect. He was supposed to graduate from high school, go to university, find a job, get married, live a happy life. I was supposed to watch him do all that. And now there was nothing. We had nothing. We were nothing. This cannot be possible; this is a nightmare. This is not real.

• • •

"BEN!" I CRY out.

I hear his heavy steps coming up the stairs two by two. I'm sorry I scared him.

"The note! Bring me the note!"

He stands in the doorway of the bedroom.

"Why do you want it now?"

I shake my head.

"I forget what he said. I want to read it again. I don't remember his writing. I want to touch the last thing that he touched."

Ben walks out to the hallway and returns a few moments later. He sits next to me and hands me a folded piece of paper. It's the original, not the photocopy the police left us after explaining that our home was considered a crime scene. His room, a crime scene. I shake my head to banish that unbelievable phrase from my mind.

My eyes are brewing another storm. I have trouble unfolding the letter. Ben is silent beside me, his blue eyes fixed on the peeling wall. Everything around us is ailing.

I lift the paper to the light — my gaze, my breath suspended.

The Raincoat

I LIKE THAT nobody stares at you; it's considered impolite. People here are very discreet, regardless of how you look. When somebody gets on the streetcar with a hot dog in hand and the whole carriage starts reeking of onions, nobody objects. When someone gets on who looks like they haven't had a bath in three months, the more sensitive people — at most — might change seats. But that's as far as it goes. So when I come in and spray alcohol on my seat, no one minds, at least not openly. I used to disinfect my spot with vinegar before, you know? I grew up believing that organic is better, and white vinegar is not only safe but cheap. People tend to react better to the smell of alcohol, though. Instead of pretending they don't notice what I'm doing, some even stretch out their hands for me to spray them, like you did, and that brings me so much joy! These days, I'll wrap myself in any silver lining life throws my way. Disinfecting my seat might give me a chance to talk to someone. And if I'm lucky, we can talk about more than just the weather.

We don't talk about the weather back where I come from. No one cares about the weather unless it's hurricane season or there's a drought. But here, people can talk about the weather forever. I'll take it if I have to, but I much prefer talking about other things. More important things, if you know what I mean. Like my yellow raincoat, for example. Thanks for asking about it! It's nice to have someone who'll talk to me instead of simply staring.

It's not easy to live alone, so far away from home. Not that I don't consider this city my home; don't get me wrong, please. I do. But if the streetcar is too crowded and I cannot grab a seat and spray it, I wait for the next one. I'm lucky I'm not like most people on the streetcar who cannot show up to work late. We all have a clock to punch, yes, but when my shift begins at rush hour, I make sure to arrive an hour early, and sometimes more, just so I don't have to pull myself in against the mass of people the driver has allowed in as the door closes behind me. You never know who has them, so you cannot be too careful. So I wait and hop on the next car, which is usually not far behind, because instead of co-ordinating with each other to pass at regular intervals, the drivers like to play elephants and keep their streetcars together in groups of two or three, as if one was holding the other's tail with its trunk. That's just what the streetcars are: elephants. Slow, huge, and heavy. Actually, given how old they were when I first arrived, I've always thought they were like mammoths. In cities like this, where you have to go to work in thirty degrees below zero, you get used to anything... even to riding a mammoth.

One thing I've noticed that does get an annoyed look out of people is a crying baby. As if it's the baby's fault that it's wrapped up so tight that it doesn't have enough air to breathe, or in one of those modern wraparounds where mothers have their kids hanging off them like an accessory to match their handbag and shoes. Only the smallest of strollers fits into one of these old streetcars. Who knows why they're still making the rounds. Lucky I don't have kids and I don't plan to. It would be a nightmare living here with kids if you had to go anywhere. Better to have a dog. Dogs here get smiled at and fussed over. People who never speak a word suddenly get up and ask, "What's his name?" or cry out, "How cute!" with a sweetness and a high-pitched squeal that is beyond bearable. The dogs aren't even that nice, really. Although sometimes I think in my next life I'd like to be one of those little pampered dogs that wear winter boots. It must be a great life. I'll bet they eat better than a lot of people I know here, or back in my country, or in a lot of other places I've never even seen.

No, I'm not complaining; it's a nice city. It's got its great big tower that I always like looking at in the night; it's so pretty. The lake that's as big as a sea. It's great, really. But I don't know if you've heard about the plague — no, not the virus. I'm talking about the silent plague that no one has been able to eradicate for decades and is only getting worse. You haven't heard? I'm not surprised. There don't even seem to be any problems here, right? That always happens in these countries where there's plenty of everything: you see the good and don't even notice the bad until it bites you, for real. My dad came from Mexico one time to visit me and he said: "Ay, my girl, this place is too clean; it can't be healthy. You're going to get sick." And naturally, since I'd only been here a short time, I treated him like he was ignorant, like he had no idea. But he was right. Then I realized that the people here are allergic to everything. There are all kinds of things they can't eat. You get a job here and pretty soon they're warning you not to bring this or that for lunch because somebody could die from so much as smelling a peanut. Now tell me, in any poor country who has ever died from smelling a peanut? Nobody. Between hunger, floods, and dust storms, nobody could ever allow themselves such luxurious allergies.

Then, when I went to the market with my dad to do the shopping and we were looking at the meat trays, searching for a steak to fry, he said to me: "Look, my girl, they only sell half the cow here. What do they do with the other half? Where's the good stuff?" I didn't know at the time, so I couldn't answer him. But later I found out that the other half of the cow is sold to the Asian markets and to the people who make dog food. Didn't I tell you that the dogs here have a great life?

Ah, but I got off track there. I was talking about the plague. Nobody talks about it; it's too embarrassing. That's why I told you before that you never know who has them, so you cannot be too careful. They're called *chinches*, or bedbugs in English. And there's a lot of them. Never in my life have I seen a bedbug, but I've seen fleas and lice, and that's enough for me, thankyouverymuch. My mother used to pick up stray animals off the street near our home, and they were always flea-ridden. She would douse them in detergent and then pluck out the fleas one by one. She'd crush them between her fingernails, crunching them and putting them together in piles of ten, because she liked to count them and then tell us how "the poor kitty had seventy-eight fleas." And then one time, one of my brothers got lice and she shaved our heads, and I'll never forget how cold I felt for weeks, or how ugly I felt until my hair no longer looked like a startled cactus and began to grow out again. No, those bugs have more than my respect; I'm terrified of them. And bedbugs are as tough as cockroaches, only in miniature. Nothing can kill them. It's been in all the newspapers, but nobody seems to care. Perhaps it's because they're mostly a PPP. You know what I mean? No? PPP: "poor-person-problem." Everyone goes on like nothing's happening because they think that if they live in a nice, clean place—one of those expensive homes it would take a family like mine five generations to finish paying off— they're out of danger. But they're wrong.

Back where I come from, you don't see rich people on the subway. Here, however, they sit down wearing their fancy suits, pretending to work or sleep, and when I watch them, I'm always thinking to myself: Don't they know the danger they're in? The danger we're *all* in? Bedbugs are contagious. You could be just standing next to someone who's got them, and *pow*! The little devils will leap onto you and make you their lifelong home. They take over the mattress on your bed, your chairs and sofas. Hell, they even get into your books and inside your electrical outlets.

Once, a woman who waited tables at the same place as me told me that they'd invaded her, and she had to vacuum everything right up to the ceiling every day and fumigate four or five times but she still hadn't gotten rid of them. She thought they'd jumped her on the subway or the streetcar, because they can hide in the fabric of the seats and then cling onto your clothes. I almost fainted from shock when she told me. No! I quit that job right away. I didn't even say goodbye to anyone. I boiled the clothes I was wearing that day as soon as I got home and I stood under the shower with the hot water running until my hands were wrinkled. And that was when this idea occurred to me.

To tell you the truth, this is the first time someone has asked me. I kept this yellow raincoat from the time I took my dad to Niagara when he came to visit. I didn't want to throw it out because it reminded me of my dad and the fun we'd had getting drenched behind the Falls, watching all that water pouring down endlessly. My father's visit has been the highlight of my time here. Don't get me wrong, I'm happy. I make more money here in a day than I'd do back home in a month. And people are nice. Polite. But sometimes I miss the easiness with which I used to make new friends before. Polite isn't warm. Polite doesn't necessarily mean to be truly welcoming. And it certainly doesn't make you feel like you belong. In all the jobs I've had—and I've had plenty, believe me, since I arrived, all of them minimum wage and with no benefits, but who am I to complain when foreign doctors are driving taxis around the streets—people have been kind, but no one has ever expected an honest answer when they ask, "How are you?" One day I was feeling homesick and I said I was feeling homesick, and I could see my colleague's mix of surprise and discomfort on her face. She said she was sorry to hear that. She said she understood, that she could imagine how hard it must be to go without the wonderful food I grew up eating, and why didn't I go try the new restaurant on such-and-such? But when you're homesick it's not only about the food, it's about the sunshine, the familiar noise on the streets. It's about the shared experience. Here, you wake up, get yourself ready for work, hop on public transit to get to work, do what you're supposed to do for seven hours and then go back home, and you can count your blessings if someone at work wants to grab lunch with you. And to everyone else, you're invisible.

But they're not invisible to me. I check people out. I see if they're scratching. If they are wearing long sleeves in the summer. I look behind their ears. What do you mean, why? Searching for bedbug bites, of course! People try to hide them, that's why you must always be suspicious. That's why I'm always very picky about who I sit next to on the streetcar.

But you were asking me about my yellow raincoat. It's a good thing that I didn't throw it out after my father and I visited the Falls, because now I wear it whenever I go out. And I've got more of them, because I went back there just to ask the tourists coming off the boat to give me theirs, and a lot of them did. I have about fifteen of the blue ones, but my favourite is this yellow one. It's the one I wear on special occasions. Whenever I'm out in the street I wear a raincoat, regardless of the weather. I keep my hair tucked up under the hood so that no bedbugs or lice can clamber onto me, and I cover my clothes with the plastic as best I can. The rubber boots are to protect the cloth of my trousers, just in case a bedbug tries to jump at me from some other pair of pants. These streetcars get really crowded at rush hour, and even if you've managed to grab a seat and spray it, you still can't be too careful. I don't want to scare you, you said you just got here and, well, how are you going to know if nobody tells you? So now you know, and you also know why I'm dressed like this in an August heatwave.

Today is a special day; that's why I'm dressed in yellow. I'm starting a new job—cleaning up the changing rooms and around the pool at a community centre. It's the perfect place for me: full of children who're learning to swim, families having fun together. Plus, I deliberately searched for a job where there'd be water and chlorine to protect me from the plague. Are you itching yet? You are, aren't you? Sometimes it can make you itch just thinking about those bugs—it's incredible. You know what I just realized? The next stop is mine! I'm going to start moving towards the door, okay? Excuse me. Oh, and welcome to Toronto!

Broken

AFTER

"FLIGHT NUMBER...to New York, now boarding at gate..." She doesn't pay attention to the announcements. They don't speak to her. "Flight number...to New York, all passengers now boarding at gate..." New York. An imaginary place, far away—could be on a different planet for all she cares. She's not travelling anywhere. All she has is this, the present. The sound of that feminine, robotic voice in the background. The noise of people walking, suitcases rolling. Lights that are always on, day and night. She'd have lost track of time if it weren't for the newspaper stands, where she can see the date on the front pages. She tries to avoid the headlines but ends up scanning them every morning.

MAN SUES POLICE DEPARTMENT, WANTS RANSOM MONEY BACK. 11-YEAR-OLD GIRL FOUND RAPED AND MURDERED, 159TH VICTIM SO FAR THIS YEAR. LOCAL SOCCER TEAM WINS CHAMPIONSHIP, FANS CELEBRATE WITH CITYWIDE CHAOS. NEW LAMBORGHINI HITS TOP SPEEDS OF 350 KM/H. ALL YOU NEED TO KNOW ABOUT THE CITY'S TRENDIEST CLUBS AND HOW TO DRESS FOR THEM.

Every hour of every day feels the same to her, except in the early morning, when the terminal is empty and she finds it easier to be at peace. The only way to know if it is raining outside is if there are wet footprints on the tiles, but even that can be tricky as the floor is cleaned constantly with wide, dirty mops that look like dead dogs.

She has made it her mission to stand guard at arrivals, but she's happiest when she's in the departures area. People are more likely to cry there. Their tears give her a chance to blend in, to stop feeling so alone.

Remembering Sylvia's words, she forces herself to believe she's safe here. She walks from one end of the airport to the other, looking around for the right person to listen to her as she pulls the suitcase she took from Sylvia's house. Hour after hour under the interminable blinding light.

BEFORE

THEY WERE BEAUTIFUL, my shoes. A present from my daughter, Alma, to wear to her high-school graduation ceremony. I bought her a lovely red dress, and she gave me the shoes, and that made her proud. She had been saving up from her weekend job at the market in order to go to teachers' college. She dreamed of improving our lives.

"You cannot come to my graduation wearing *chanclas*, Mother," she said, looking at my flip-flops with contempt. My feet were not used to wearing proper shoes, let alone high heels, and I complained the instant I put them on.

"Come on, *mija*. I look like a fat chicken trying to balance on a cactus."

Alma laughed. The sound soft and fresh, like a shy waterfall.

"They're not that high," she reassured me. "You'll get used to them. You'll just have to start wearing them now so you're ready on graduation day." And she waved her index finger at me as if issuing a serious warning, her smile a big ray of sunshine on her face.

I promised I would, and I honestly tried, but back then I thought to myself, Who can work cleaning jobs wearing fancy shoes? Screw this. I told her I was wearing them, and I did, once. I decided I would walk very slowly on her big night and then forget about the damned shoes, keep them in a drawer as a nice memento to show my grandchildren: "Your momma insisted on me wearing *theeeese* on her graduation night, can you imagine?" And I pictured two or three little faces laughing with me. I fantasized a little, imagining their gender, looking for names that would suit them. What would Alma call her children? She had grown up so fast! I knew she wanted to pursue a career and be independent, but I couldn't wait to hold a little hand in mine again. I had always yearned for a large family. Destiny had something else in mind. I hoped it would be different for Alma.

DURING

YOU WALK EVERYWHERE with leaflets, carrying a big cardboard sign, showing people her picture and asking each and every one who crosses your path if they've seen her. Some don't even bother to take a good look; others say the first thing they can think of to make you feel better: "I've seen her. Do you go to the church around the corner? I think I remember her from last Sunday's Mass." But you haven't been to Mass since your parents disowned you and the priest said single mothers were not welcome in Heaven, so you say thanks and keep searching. You scout your entire neighbourhood, venturing down streets you didn't even know were there, trying not to twist your ankle or be run over as you walk on uneven dirt roads without sidewalks. The roads of the poor.

You have been to the police, the hospitals, the government offices, the morgue. "My name is Adela Ramírez. My daughter, Alma, is missing. Seventeen years old, brunette, medium-length wavy hair, skinny, not very tall but very outspoken." People behind desks pretend to care as they scribble down a few notes and promise you they'll look into it. A file has been opened, but you know that doesn't mean something will be done. So you dress up, wear your new shoes hoping they will summon your child back, hoping that if people see you well-dressed they will want to help, take you seriously, give you an appointment with someone higher up. But new shoes or no new shoes, they don't have time to hear you out again or they tell you useless things like, she'll come back did you have a fight with her she must have run away all teenagers are like that just be patient perhaps she had a different boyfriend she didn't tell you about just go home and take care of yourself trust the Lord leave her picture here again we will call you if we hear anything there's no need for you to come back we're on it and we're so sorry, which only proves what you've always known: when you're no one, you're no one. And so is your child.

You cannot think straight because you don't sleep. All you do is scream and cry and beg, wishing to hold your child in your arms again. Little things trigger huge storms within your chest. The childhood hairclips shaped like rubber duckies that your little girl, your happy girl, wore every day in grade four. A clean, lonely sock sitting on the dresser waiting patiently for its match to reappear. Her pyjamas, which still smell like her lavender body lotion, which you dare not wash, hoping life is like a movie and some dog will come and sniff them and lead you to her. But life is not a movie.

You have bills to pay, so you keep your evening job cleaning an office in order to go looking for your child during the day, every day, because you know no one else will do it. You barely eat, forget to shower, and wish you could disappear as well. You snap at those who try to comfort you: Would *you* be able to calm down? You ache for your child's long fingers and dirty plates and mood swings — her driving you crazy with her presence, not her absence. You want to tell her she's the best thing that ever happened to you, beg her forgiveness for everything you've ever done wrong. Different scenarios play in your head of how things could have been done differently so that this would never have happened.

You're an open wound oozing despair. You become a sickness.

• • •

IT'S A ONE-STOREY house surrounded by a high wall crowned with pieces of broken glass, a common and cheap way to feel protected against intruders. The garage door and the front door are made of metal. As they pull into the entrance, Adela notices the sidewalk, narrow and crooked, and feels sorry for the scrawny tree that has managed to survive despite being surrounded by concrete. The house has no windows visible from the outside.

Sylvia: You can stay here as long as you want.

Adela (fighting back tears): I don't know how to thank you.

Sylvia (getting out of the car to open the garage door): Don't worry.

Adela studies Sylvia's movements. Before getting out of the car, she checks her surroundings, makes sure there is nobody on the street. When she's satisfied, she opens the garage — the door screeches — and then returns to the car to drive it inside.

Sylvia: You can never be too careful.

Adela nods. She feels the urge to cry but holds back. Such a clever, brave young woman. The first one to really take an interest in Alma's disappearance. And an important person, too. A journalist.

Sylvia closes the garage door and helps Adela bring in her belongings. She was not allowed to take anything except her clothes and her daughter's treasures: pictures, crafts, a few books, some partially used makeup, inexpensive jewellery, a half-finished bottle of perfume, and a doll. Her high-school diploma and final report card, which her friends brought to Adela in sealed envelopes that she has not had the strength to open. The barely worn high-heeled shoes and the never-worn red dress. It all fits into a couple of boxes and a black garbage bag.

Sylvia (opening the front door, which has three different locks): What they did to you was unfair and wrong. We'll fight them, you'll see.

Adela: All I care about is finding my daughter.

Sylvia (pushing open the door and turning on the lights): I know. But for your landlord to kick you out because you couldn't pay the rent—and then to keep your furniture and stuff as payment is wrong. Almost criminal under the circumstances.

Adela (following Sylvia into the house): I tried to keep my night job; I really did.

Sylvia (closing the door and turning the key on all three locks): After what you've been through, it's understandable. And you shouldn't be expected to, either. This country is fucked up. The world needs to hear about it.

It is a modest but cozy house. Adela thinks it would be cozier if there were not so many stacks of papers on the tables in the dining room and the living room, on the sofa and chairs. Sylvia leads Adela down a hallway into a small room with a twin bed and a night table. There's a small closet and a window that looks onto a patio that has no grass or flowers.

Sylvia (smiling): This will be your room. I hope you're comfortable.

Adela breaks down.

AFTER

IN THE COURSE *of one day the adult heart will beat more than 86,000 times. In one year, more than 31 million times. By age seventy, a human heart will have logged upwards of 2.3 billion contractions.* Someone had left one of those magazines for women on a chair. She picks it up, thinking she'll find some distraction looking at the pictures of makeup she'd never wear but would have looked great on Alma. Instead, she finds an article written by a lady whose baby had a heart defect and died a few days after birth. It gets Adela thinking about how lucky that mother was, being able to cuddle her child as he died. Having a grave to visit. She does the count with the calculator on her phone, and finds out that Alma's heart beat around 682 million times up until the last day she saw her. Sylvia's heart stopped at around 1.6 billion.

Large numbers; short lives.

BEFORE

A MONTH BEFORE her graduation, Alma called to let me know she'd leave the house in the early afternoon and come back for dinner after finishing a last-minute assignment with her classmates. I thought it was odd that she hadn't asked them to come over, which is what they always did. With me gone all day and into the evening at work, they had our small apartment to themselves and they liked that.

"Why can't they come over?" I asked.

"It's more convenient this way," she stated, trying to appear nonchalant. But her voice gave her away. She was lying.

"Are you going to see Bobby?"

She didn't answer.

"Are you?" I asked again.

She still didn't answer.

"He's a bartender, *mija*. A loser. Why can't you understand that?"

"He's not a loser."

I remembered myself at her age, falling in love with her deadbeat father, and my heart sank.

"Do you want to ruin your life like I did?"

I didn't mean to say that. It came out wrong.

"So *I* ruined your life?" She replied bitterly.

I tried to explain what I meant, but she hung up and didn't pick up again when I called back. By the time I came home that evening she still wasn't there.

DURING

SHE WAS WEARING blue jeans, a white T-shirt, and the bright yellow sneakers she had bought at the market just the previous weekend. You figure it out after you go through her closet to see what is missing. Along with her.

You call her cell phone tirelessly but it goes straight to voicemail every time. You call her friends but they haven't seen her. You call Bobby at the bar where he works, but he says she didn't show up for their date. He claims to have called her and been sent straight to voicemail. To your surprise, he comes over right away to offer you support. He's there when you call the police, helps you make the first flyers to post around the neighbourhood, and spreads the word on social media.

#Missing

You're hopeful until you see how many other pleas for help like yours are online. Little girls, teenage girls, girls of all ages reported missing, disappeared, kidnapped. Vanished. Boys too, but mostly girls.

You don't understand: you taught your daughter to be careful, to take good care of herself. She was never out alone after dark, she had her phone at all times, she always told you where she was going and with whom. What else could you have done?

If you paid attention to everything the news says you'd never dare leave the house. You cannot stop living your life. Weren't those your words?

But it's the last words you uttered, the last words she heard from you, that kill you.

It's your fault.

AFTER

ADELA HAS A routine. Around midnight, she lies down on the floor in a far corner of the terminal. There are always a few passengers here and there, sleeping in a chair or resting against a wall, waiting for an early flight, so she hasn't found it hard to pretend she's one of them. She ties her suitcase to her wrist to make sure no one steals it while her eyes are closed, and tries to rest until dawn, when she heads to the family washroom and locks herself in. There, she opens up her suitcase and checks that everything is in order.

Sylvia's documents, the ones she took from the secret spot behind the pantry.

Alma's red dress at the very bottom, her baby pictures,

her PJs. The lavender smell of her body has almost faded. Adela's stomach churns.

Once she has gone over her inventory, she gets ready to clean herself and wash her clothes in the sink: top, underwear, and socks only. Drying jeans under the hand dryer is nearly impossible, so she has decided to wear them until her job is done. Her hair is short, easy to wash under the faucet; she doesn't have to spend too much money on toiletries. A shower would be nice, but sponge baths are better than nothing. She avoids looking at herself in the mirror for too long. She has lost weight, dark circles have formed under her eyes, and her hair has gone completely grey. Soon she will have to find herself a job; the money Sylvia left her is running low. But she doesn't want to think about that just yet.

She has a mission.

BEFORE

"MOM, WHY DID you call me Alma?"

It was Sunday and I was cooking eggs for breakfast. Alma was sitting at the kitchen table, eating a banana.

"Because from the moment you were born, I knew you were a special soul, and my biggest love."

She wrinkled her nose.

"Do you have to be so corny?"

I laughed.

"I wish you had named me Pamela."

I stopped paying attention to the eggs and turned around to look at her, genuinely curious and surprised.

"Why?"

She shrugged.

"Dunno. Sounds fancier. And definitely not corny."

I smiled, put the eggs on our plates, and brought them to the table.

"I didn't like my name when I was your age, either," I said, trying to make her feel better.

"Really? Why?" she asked, taking her first bite.

"The song. 'Y si Adelita se fuera con otro...' Children at school used to make fun of me," I lied.

Alma started singing "Adelita" at the top of her lungs. I covered my ears with my hands, and we both burst into laughter.

I didn't tell her the truth—the real reason why I didn't like my name. The song is about a girl whose lover is willing to follow her by train or by ship, even if she leaves him for someone else, because he cannot live without her. I grew up thinking my name held a promise. Alma's father used to sing it into my ear when we were together.

Then he left.

DURING

AFTER THE FIRST few weeks, during which people help you distribute leaflets and hug you when they see you, they go back to their lives, their routines. Their concern turns into pity and then into oblivion. You become part of the country's gruesome statistics. And they avoid you even though they know your face, your name, your child, and your story. At first you are enraged. Do they think, deep down, that your girl deserved whatever it was that happened to her? That she went looking for it? Or that it happened because you were never there? Always working, single mother, no family or close friends to help raise that child, how irresponsible of you. Then you realize they're only trying to cope. You've made it feel too close to home for them. They're afraid of becoming you.

A decision has to be made. You choose to continue your search alone. After a sleepless night, you leave the house early to catch a bus that will take you out of the city. You get off near the highway, then start walking downhill. It's going to be a hot day. It hasn't rained in weeks. All you can hear is the sound of your own steps. The air feels heavy and your mouth is dry, but you have to save your water, so you just moisten your lips with your tongue. After a few minutes you hear voices. Female voices. Then you see them. A handful of women walking with long iron rods, sticks, and shovels, searching the ground. They all wear hats—you'll bring one tomorrow, you tell yourself—and colourful handkerchiefs around their necks whose purpose, you learn later on, is to cover their noses and mouths in case someone finds what they all dread but are desperately looking for.

These women are well organized and immediately welcome you into their fold. They too have been ignored by the authorities—their pleas dismissed, their files buried under hundreds of others collecting dust on some bureaucrat's desk. Loss has brought them together; they have even given their group a name: Colectivo del Monte.

This is the worst club anyone can belong to.

Mothers of the Disappeared.

AFTER

ADELA CANNOT BELIEVE how unsuccessful she's been trying to find the kind of person Sylvia told her to look for, but she forces herself to keep trying.

A family of four is coming through the sliding doors. They appear tired but happy. Mother, father, a teenage girl, and a young boy. Adela doesn't understand a word they're saying, but she doesn't care. She approaches the man without hesitation.

"*Perdone, Señor, ¿habla español?*"

The man and his family seem surprised at her bold-
ness. They're looking for someone to help them carry their
suitcases. He tries to wave her away with his hand. Adela
gives the foreign woman a pleading glance that catches
her attention. The teenage girl rolls her eyes. The boy says
something that sounds like, "Can we go now?"

"No queremos comprar nada."

He has a heavy accent but evidently speaks the language.
Adela looks him in the eyes, pleading.

"Are you a journalist?"

BEFORE

"HOW WAS YOUR day?"

That's how Alma and I always greeted each other when
we came home. I almost never told her the truth about my
days. Cleaning motel rooms is hard work. People are filthy.
I found all sorts of disgusting things on the bedsheets: boog-
ers, blood stains, vomit, sweat, semen, pubic hair, nails,
fleas. We had a certain amount of time to clean each room,
so I did the best I could, but I developed a chronic repug-
nance for these places. When Alma asked why we never
went on vacations like some of her classmates, I made up
excuses like, the beach is only a couple of hours away we
always go there to spend the day when you feel like it we
really do not need more than that we don't have much

money we must save up for your education, but she kept insisting, she wanted to go to the capital, to see the big city.

Alma was such a bright student. When she was about to turn fifteen, I went to a travel agency and got some brochures, which I hid at the very bottom of my purse, and studied them when Alma was not around. Finally, I made up my mind, chose an itinerary, and was ready to book it as a surprise for her. I was in a very good mood that day, humming a Shakira song that played on the radio all the time.

When I entered the last room I was supposed to clean before lunch, I immediately knew something was wrong. The red stain on the bed was too large. I didn't dare to look for what had caused it. I called the manager instead.

The police came. An ambulance was not necessary.

They found a girl—well, she would have been a girl if only she had been allowed to be born.

After the officers had finished taking everyone's testimony, they took the bedding as evidence. The mattress was stained; the blood had seeped in. I watched as the manager and the security guard turned it over, then I was asked to get the room ready for the next guest.

"How was your day?" Alma asked me that evening when I came home.

I broke down as I held her tight against my chest. The next morning, I tore the brochures into little pieces.

No sleeping away from home for us.

DURING

LIKE EVERY DAY for the past few weeks, you comb through the thirsty soil as it drinks up the thick drops of sweat falling from your forehead. The mothers had decided to search the hill from the bottom up. You're already close to the top, so your rod seems heavier than before. It's sunny. The heat makes your clothes stick to your skin. You've been told what to look for if there's no smell to guide you. Swarms of flies. Cigarette butts. Food wrappers. Empty beer bottles. Cans. Anything that suggests a human presence in this ungrateful landscape might be a sign.

A scream pierces the air. The voice stabs you in the stomach and you cannot move. You're paralyzed with fear. It's only when you see the rest of the mothers heading to the source of the scream that you react and start walking. Your feet feel impossibly heavy. Your knees are weak.

"Cover your mouth with the handkerchief!" someone warns you. As you approach the group, the stench hits you. A woman is bent over, crying. The others are standing next to her, trying to comfort her, teary as well.

"That's my son's shoe," she says, pointing to the ground.

You look. There's a white something showing through the dirt...How does she know it's his shoe? you wonder. Then again, you'd recognize your daughter's sneakers immediately, wouldn't you?

"Don't touch anything. I'll call the cops," someone says, and you stand still. Who knows how many more bodies are here? Every day, the news reports the discovery of new clandestine graves containing human remains. And now you know it's true; you're seeing it with your own eyes. The entire country is turning into a graveyard. Who knows what you're standing on, what's waiting for you in the earth? What if Alma's here? The thought makes you dizzy.

It seems like hours until the forensic team arrives. They cordon off the area, make you walk away. You watch from a distance as they dig. You refuse to go home. You refuse to eat or drink. You're just standing there, under the sun, your heart barely beating.

You wake up at the hospital. You don't know her yet, but Sylvia is sitting by your side. She offers you water and introduces herself. She wants to hear your story, but when you try to talk, you find no words inside you, just wails.

ADELA IS PREPARING Sylvia's favourite dish when the phone rings. She runs from the kitchen to the landline in the hallway.

Adela (picking up the phone): Hello?

Man (muffled, angry voice): Listen to me, you cunt! Tell that bitch that we warned her to be quiet, but she fucked up real bad.

Adela: Who is this?

Gunshots are heard in the distance. Adela drops the phone, hunkers down, and covers her ears, shaking.

AFTER

ADELA FEELS LIKE she has hit the jackpot. The man she intercepted is a journalist and his expression softens as she explains herself. He seems interested in hearing her story now. As he translates for his family, they appear to warm to her.

A geyser has erupted inside Adela's mouth. They move their luggage to the side, look for a spot to sit down away from the crowd.

Trying as best as she can not to break down, she tells them about Alma's disappearance. About how her clothes were found on the body of another girl and no one could offer an explanation as to how that could happen, other than "They sometimes do that in order to confuse the police." She talks about Sylvia and her investigation into the disappearance of dozens of people leading all the way up to a drug cartel linked to the governor and the chief of police. She can tell by the man's gaze that he believes her. The woman wipes away a few tears.

The man signals for Adela to wait while he makes a phone call. His cautious words blend with the robotic female voice in the background announcing flight departures, the footsteps of people coming and going, and the roller suitcases grinding past them. After weeks of leaping from memory to memory, trying to hold the pieces of her shattered life together, Adela feels something like relief. Is this what hope feels like? She shakes her head: she cannot afford to let her guard down just yet. In this country, where brave journalists like Sylvia are murdered every day, where women's lives mean nothing, where mothers' pain means nothing, where she herself, and Alma, are nobodies in an ocean of dead and missing and grieving nobodies, hope is not the last thing to die, but the first. The real fight, she knows — the one for justice — is just about to begin.

The General's Daughter

HER NAME WAS Polita and we pronounced it *Poll-ee-tah*, but I do not know what it was short for or how she spelled it. I never asked. Polita was slightly younger than me, and when I met her, Mother pinched my arm and gave me *the look*, the one that screamed that I was being bad, so I checked myself to find out what I was doing that I wasn't supposed to. I was standing straight, as if balancing a book on my head. Check. I had said "hello" nicely. Check. My blouse was clean, starched, and ironed and there wasn't a speck of dirt on my skirt (God forbid the daughter of a general should wear stained clothes). Check. My patent-leather shoes were shiny. Check. And my hair in place, neatly braided with the help of slimy pink gel—the stuff Mother bought especially because she couldn't stand my frizz, couldn't stand the way the short hairs rose up on their own even after she had combed back my mane: small rebellious warriors mocking a military salute. If only I were like my brother, Oscar! If only I had taken after Mother's mother, and not Father's! But science has proven that good genes are the weakest, and everyone has a cross to bear, and my hair was Mother's cross. My hair, and the heat and humidity, which made the situation worse. When I was five years old, she had my entire head shaved, hoping I would grow new —*please-God-make-it-straight!*— hair. But when my Medusa strands started re-sprouting like a sickness, she avoided me for days. Then, on my sixth birthday, she made a grand entry into my room, the pink gel a new weapon in her hand, and made it her mission to braid my hair every morning, dragging it back and brushing it down until it was tame and crunchy, until my head hurt and my eyes were pulled out of shape. So if posture, dress, shoes, and braids were fine, what had I done when I met Polita that earned me a pinch and *the look*?

I had been staring. Staring, yet blinded by the black sun of her curls.

Oscar was thirteen and I, eight. Mother had had two miscarriages between us. Sometimes when she looked at me and tried to smile, I knew she was yearning for those lost babies. Her unborn, straight-haired babies. Instead she had me, my paternal grandmother reborn: I saw the world through the almonds of her very same eyes; my hair twirled to the rhythm of the riot breeding on her scalp. Father had straight hair too, and Mother was already his fiancée by the time she met her mother-in-law, the wedding carefully planned, too late for her to back out on her dream of becoming a general's wife.

I was a punishment for her arrogance. But I didn't deserve to be.

MEMORIES OF MY childhood include sitting in the tub with Oscar, taking a bath together, our hair white with shampoo, and then Mother rinsing our heads before helping him to get out, dry up, dress, and brush, while I sat in the now lukewarm water waiting for the conditioner to work its magic so the comb could slide through without drawing tears. Those baths ended when Oscar turned eleven and he got an erection. I didn't know what it was but understood the severity of the situation as soon as Mother yelled at me. I was not supposed to make him do that, dirty little girl! She slapped me. Her hand hurt more when it was wet. I was only six, but I remember his penis, its swollen head, the honey-coloured fuzz that fenced it in. I remember Mother scrubbing me on the outside as if she could reach my insides to clean them, too. And I remember how Oscar stared at me after that evening. But he did not get *the look* or a pinch. Instead—and I found this out much later—Mother asked Father to do something about Oscar. Father did what fathers do: he paid a woman to help Oscar become a man. I wasn't sure what was going on, but some feral instinct told me to lock my bedroom door. Mother disapproved.

Your bedroom will be too hot at night if you close your door, she said. Besides, we have nothing to hide.

FATHER SAW THAT I was lonely and decided I needed a friend. I did not get along with the girls at school. Mother was proud to be the General's wife, and had instilled that same pride in me, but the girls at school did not want to include the General's daughter in their games. I did not understand why. Mother said it was because they envied me. They envied our house, with its cool marble floors and ceiling fans. The fact that Father had all those medals and a driver assigned especially to his personal service. Private Domínguez, who we all addressed by his last name only. I believed her; what else was I supposed to do?

I was told we lived in a blessed land that some bad men and women had wanted to take over. Father had helped to save it, so our people would remain united and at peace. We had to live in this town, surrounded by palm trees and infested by mosquitoes, until things went back to normal and we could move back to the capital.

It was Father's idea to hire Polita's mother to work at home. A live-in maid to help Mother around the house. And Polita would be my companion. We would play together when I came home from school. Mother protested to no avail; she already had a cleaning lady who came every day and she did not want an outsider sharing the intimacy and luxuries of our home. Father was adamant, however, so she was forced to give in. She remained firm about one thing, though: the fact that Polita's hair was allowed to grow like weed, she said, didn't mean mine would be left unbraided.

Oscar, in the meantime, had grown to be almost as tall as Father, and his voice was starting to change. So were his eyes, always fixated on everyone's butt. No, not everyone's. Women's butts. Women's boobs. I heard him making crude remarks to Domínguez when Father was not around to hear. They laughed and their sharp guffaws cut my breath. After that, I remember praying every night for God to never give me boobs.

I PLAYED WITH Polita in my room. We played dolls. We played board games — Memory was her favourite, she always won. We drew pictures. She drew herself and her mommy. She called her "Mommy" and I have forgotten what her actual name was. I remember so many things but not that, and there is no trace of her in any of the papers or files I have gone through. I remember her gentle hands, though, and her smile. If her smile had been a sound, it would have been a harp.

Polita drew her mommy, and I drew either Father and me together, or landscapes. Landscapes that depicted places and things I had only seen in books: icebergs, snow, mountains covered in pine and fir trees. Life is civilized in places with snow, Mother said. People are not slackers like they are here, because if they were, they would perish. This weather is a curse. People can be lazy good-for-nothings and thrive, but in cold climates people must be efficient. There is no room for idleness: cold weather can kill you if you do not have a house or a job. No one there lives in a hut. That is why the First World is the First World and everyone who lives there has a nice life. The cold keeps people working, doing their share. Unlike here, especially in this godforsaken town, she said, rolling her eyes. One day we would travel and see the snow. Oscar and I would see, first-hand, how civilized people lived. But that wasn't why I was drawn towards snow and landscapes. I thought they looked pretty, so white and so blue, so clean. I couldn't get enough of drawing them.

Polita too made a drawing of Father once, after he took us to the town fair. I wanted desperately to attend, but Mother complained that it was too hot to go out; she had a headache, for which she took a couple of sleeping pills. She couldn't take me. Not that she would have: before rolling over and turning her back to me, she said town fairs were for the populace—I remember the word and the nasal tone with which she sneered it.

Father had come home early that day, so despite my trepidations, I asked Domínguez to take me to the fair along with Polita. He laughed. He wasn't accepting orders from a girl. Father was so upset when I went crying to him that he made Domínguez drive us all to the fair— him, in full general's uniform; Polita, in her favourite pink Hello Kitty T-shirt, and me, wearing my favourite flowery blouse—and we spent the entire afternoon on the rides. People let us cut in line and bowed their heads to us. Father won prizes for us both: a clay pirate parrot for me and a piggy bank for Polita. She was so happy even her hair seemed to be smiling.

And when we arrived back home, he gave Polita's mother the rest of the evening off and ordered Domínguez to perform her duties. Father whispered in my ear that he wanted to teach him a lesson. No one would ever mistreat his princess. He cared for no other girl in the world.

Serve us dinner.

Yes, Sir.

This plate is cold, warm it up.

Yes, Sir.

Now it is too hot. Do you want to burn my hand?

No, Sir. Sorry, Sir.

Take it back to the kitchen.

Yes, Sir.

Clean the table.

Yes, Sir.

And wash the dishes.

Yes, Sir.

Father grinned at me in complicity; I joined him in the fun and took off my shoes.

Shine them.

Yes, Madam.

I did not so much as glance at him as I enunciated my order, but I revelled in Oscar's disapproving look. He had never been so quiet while we ate. Oh, how I relished the fact that Mother was not there!

Nyah-nyah-nyah-nyah-nyah-nyah!

ON THE AFTERNOONS when he was not receiving private training at the military base, Oscar would sit behind Polita and me in the family room while we watched the afternoon cartoons, Father's Remington 870 in his hands, and practice pulling it apart, then reassembling it again. He had started to wear Father's cologne, so much of it that I could always tell when he was coming before I heard his footsteps. I had to open up all the windows in the family room to let in some air. It was better to have the afternoon heat swallow us all up than to sit in that room suffocating in his mix of sweat and cologne.

Oscar startled us every time he slapped the table in frustration because, even though his speed was improving, he was still not as fast as Father. You trying to be like Father is like Wile E. Coyote trying to catch the Road Runner, I said to him one day. Polita burst out laughing, as did I. But my brother didn't laugh. I tried to put out the sudden fire in his eyes: Can't you take a joke? He stood up and left the room, the Remington abandoned on the table. In the background, a rock crushed the Coyote. *Beep-beep!*

OSCAR STOPPED JOINING us for a few days until one hot afternoon when, seeking solace from the heat, Polita and I were lying on our stomachs on the marble floor, watching *I Dream of Jeannie*. It was Oscar's favourite show: I had heard him tell Domínguez the genie was a true *mamacita*. You think she's blond down there, too? They had laughed, and I wished that I could cross my arms and blink like her to make his words go away. A faint discomfort grew in my stomach every time the show was on after that, but Polita loved it, so that day we were watching it as Oscar took his usual seat behind us. Right after he finished reassembling the 870 — the sound of the final push of the magazine spring retainer into the magazine tube and then its rotation was like a song I knew by heart — he slid the barrel under Polita's skirt and peeked at her underwear. I did not see him do it, but she let out a cry and jumped to her feet, scaring me. What's wrong? I thought maybe she had seen a scorpion. They were plentiful at that time of the year. But when Polita told me what Oscar had done, I couldn't believe my ears. How dare you, I yelled at him. He let out a guffaw: Can't you take a joke? Polita was making a huge effort to hold back her tears. As I wrapped my arms around her, she reminded me of the bunny rabbit Father once shot in the fields when I was little. It had still been alive when he picked it up. Father had to twist its neck to put it out of its misery.

Mother was flipping through a fashion magazine when I entered her room looking for Father. I hadn't heard him leave and wanted to tell on Oscar. I don't know what I was thinking when I decided to share with her what had just transpired. The geyser in my stomach was threatening to erupt through my eyes and mouth and I could not control it. I had to take a deep breath so my voice wouldn't shatter. Mother listened to me, then asked me to sit down next to her on the bed. Trying to placate the rebellious tiny hairs that sprouted out of my braids with one hand, and still holding her magazine with the other, she spoke gently: You'll suffer too much if you take such things seriously. Men are like that. Besides, he was only joking, right? Do you think this dress would look nice on me?

Oscar had already turned sixteen and Mother kept on tousling his hair, calling him her big man, massaging his neck and shoulders. She seemed intoxicated by him, even by the pungent, animal smell of his sweat mixed with Father's cologne that made me gag.

I tried to teach Oscar a lesson by giving him my own version of *the look* at dinner, but he ignored me.

A FEW DAYS later, I arrived home from school to find that Polita and her mother were not there. I asked Mother where they were. Gone, she said. I got tired of seeing them. I never wanted them here in the first place.

Her words were like a punch in the stomach: I bent over in half and began to cry. How could Polita leave me like that, without even saying goodbye? We had plans to do each other's nails that afternoon. I couldn't understand what was going on.

Where's Father?

Something came up and he had to leave on an unexpected trip. He'll be back in a couple of days.

I had to hold on to the table to keep my balance. Now I was Wile E. Coyote, free-falling into an abyss.

I ran to Polita's room. All of her things were gone. The drawings she had made with me, which her mommy had proudly taped to the walls for decoration, had been removed in haste; a few pieces of tape holding on to severed corners of paper were still there. So was Polita's piggy bank. That didn't make any sense. Nothing did. Mother would not tell me what had truly happened. Neither would Oscar when he finally came home from the military base. He stank of sweat and dirt but wasn't wearing any cologne for once. I looked him in the eyes and he held my gaze without blinking. Mother came out of her room to hug him as he reached the top of the stairs. You must be hungry, my love. Let me fix you something to eat.

That night, the lullaby of the cicadas was my only comfort as I cried myself to sleep.

WHEN FATHER RETURNED a few days later, Mother received him with a long kiss on the lips — it was the first time she had kissed him in front of Oscar and me — though neither of them smiled. I complained to Father as soon as he took off his forage cap.

Where's Polita? Can you please take me to see her?

He cupped my face in his hands.

Princess, didn't your mother tell you they were stealing from us?

I froze. I knew this was a lie. If they needed money so badly, why leave the piggy bank behind? Was this how Mother had convinced him to take my only friend away from me? I confronted Mother as soon as we were alone.

You want the truth?

Yes.

That woman was flirting with your father.

I don't believe you.

Men have urges, stupid child.

SOON, A NEW live-in maid arrived. She was an old, plump woman who, Mother proudly announced, was very quiet and minded her own business. I felt relieved that I had brought Polita's piggy bank into my bedroom and hidden it in the back of my closet. I decided I'd collect all the spare change I could find around the house and save it for her. I'd hand it over when I saw her. Every day on my way to school, I yearned to run into her or her mommy. Perhaps they were hiding behind a palm tree, waiting for me to pass by in Father's car? They would not want to be seen by Domínguez at the wheel, but they'd do something to make me notice them. At least Polita would. I was sure of it. Months went by before my eyes stopped scouring every sidewalk, every crosswalk for the black sun that shone on Polita's head.

• • •

THE DAY AFTER my sixteenth birthday, both my parents accompanied Oscar to get him settled into military school. Mother was eager to travel to the capital to do some shopping, she said, but I knew she really wanted to be near Oscar for as long as possible. Before getting into the car, my brother turned to look at me and gave me a military salute. I followed suit. Perhaps we would get along better when he returned for the holidays. As I waved goodbye, I wondered what life would be like with just the three of us at home. I was afraid of being Mother's only focus.

Tired of the gel and the braids, I decided to celebrate my time alone by letting my hair down and taking a long hot bath. Grandma would be proud of me if she could see me, I said to myself in front of the mirror: the chestnut explosion that framed my face was exactly like hers. I would keep my hair down until my parents' return. Perhaps Father would help me convince Mother to leave my hair alone finally? I remembered a photo of Grandma taken with Oscar, where her hair looked like a woolen blanket. I was sure that if I showed it to Father, he would help my cause. Where had I seen it last? Had Oscar taken it with him?

Hungry for that image of my grandmother, I entered Oscar's bedroom. The smell of cologne had impregnated everything: the bedding, the curtains, the rug. I held my breath as I searched the top of his dresser and his nightstand. The photo wasn't there. I let the air out of my lungs and sighed. It had to be somewhere in that room. All I had to do was keep looking. I opened his drawers one by one and was surprised by how disorganized they were. I expected better from someone who was about to become a soldier.

I had almost given up when, at the back of the bottom drawer, something caught my eye. Something that did not belong. As I pulled it towards me, my hands began to tremble. What was it doing there? Then I began to panic, my mind refusing to believe what I saw before me. Please, God, please, please, please, don't let it be. Don't let it be hers. But it was. I was holding it in my hands — hands that did not feel like my own. A stranger's hands in a stranger's room in a stranger's house. I looked around me but did not recognize anything except the small pink T-shirt with the face of Hello Kitty, staring up at me beneath dark brown stains.

Bear Hug

For Don and Jan Cross, and
for Ms. Margaret Cross, in memoriam.

I SAT THE teddy bear down in the back seat. Before gently
fastening the seat belt around it, I removed my mask and
tucked it inside my pocket. I did not want my glasses to
fog up as I stared at it for the last time. Despite taking the
best of care—first her and then me—the years had worn
it down. The plush of its fur, once velvety and a bright
shade of amber, now looked rough and opaque. We, too,
had become rough and opaque; time shows no mercy. That
infant-sized teddy had spent its days on Mother's bed and
its nights on top of her chest of drawers, always close at
hand ever since Dad had given it to her as a gift back in
1956—when they were dating—up until dementia began
gnawing at her memories and all my promises had to be
broken. That was a year ago, when we moved her into a
retirement home, which is the pleasant name we give to

a place where we drop off our elders so someone else can clean up their bodily fluids and chase away the ghosts of their pasts. I told myself I was doing it to save what was left of my own sanity.

They had been together since 1956, Mother and her bear. Sixty-three years, because the bear has lived in my apartment during this past year, deep inside my closet, zipped up in a plastic bag — I couldn't stand its odour of medicine, camphor, and mothballs, that commotion of scents that had slowly eroded my Mother's favourite perfume and taken ownership of everything that was hers. It was this same scent, however, that tore a wounded animal's wail from me when I opened the bag to retrieve the bear: Mother's essence had condensed itself in those rounded ears and that pointy nose, crowned with a plastic button that had been threatening to fall off since who knows when. That teddy bear was all I had left of her. All I had left of Father, too. Without it, I'd be a complete orphan. What a ridiculous idea for a woman my age, I thought; it's nothing more than an object. An object Mother talked to when she thought she was alone; an object she loved even more, perhaps, than me.

Sixty-three years. I took out my phone to do the math. Sixty-three times three hundred and sixty-five (I skipped leap years to make it easier): 22,990 days and nights of companionship. Of course, she should have celebrated her silver, gold, and diamond wedding anniversaries with Father; instead, she held a teddy bear.

As if commenting on my grief, at that very moment a plane crossed the sky above me. Its sound startled me. I had been inured to the sound of ambulances only. Why hadn't they closed the airport along with the border? How come they were still letting people in and out of the country on airplanes, as if things were normal? Who in the world takes an airplane, and even more so during these times? Mother would have said the same thing, without adding "these times." The lack of confidence—no, not the lack of confidence, the contempt—she felt towards airplanes, instead of diminishing, had increased as she aged.

And she aged from one day to the next after Father's death. Her hair became grizzled, and she didn't have the strength to get out of bed for days. I couldn't sleep thinking about what I'd do if I lost her, too. I had to beg her to eat—sandwiches, which was all I knew how to make, and all we had for several days after the leftover food from the funeral ran out. I walked to school and came home every day to find her in the same position, under the covers, her eyes red from crying. One night I had a nightmare and I ran to Mother's bed seeking comfort, but she turned her back on me.

"Go away. Eventually, you'll leave me, too," she said in a soft yet bitter voice.

"I won't ever leave you, Mom. What are you talking about?" I did not understand. Couldn't she see that I needed her? I had lost my father, too. I missed hearing his steps down the hallway after he said goodnight to me. I missed the three of us, together, living our everyday lives. Pouring cereal in a bowl in the morning, getting ready to start the day. Playing Chinese checkers on the weekend. Walking to the park. Feeling protected.

"Children grow up and leave. I'll be all alone."

It was only after I promised that I'd never leave her that she finally turned around and took me in her arms, and we cried ourselves to sleep. It took me years to realize the weight she had thrust upon my shoulders that night. She also made me swear I'd never set foot on board an airplane.

"At least you managed to keep *that* promise," she reminded me as we watched the reports of the terrorist attack in New York on September eleventh. "You should thank me."

I was living on my own but within walking distance from her place, and we had dinner together every night. But that wasn't enough. Nothing I did was ever enough. She was never happy again after Father's death. I can still picture her shaking her head in front of the television as she cursed between her teeth.

"How many more widows, how many more orphans until people finally realize?" Her words lingered in the late-summer air, which smelled of Guerlain's "Shalimar," her favourite — and also Rita Hayworth's, whom apparently she had resembled in her youth. Or at least, so Father used to say.

It was useless to argue with Mother or try to show her statistics. The numbers that proved that travelling by airplane was safer than travelling by any other means meant nothing to her. She compared them to what was tangible, the only item we had recovered from Father: his half-burnt passport. There had been looting at the site of the crash, that's why we didn't recover his wallet. It was stolen. No one was ever apprehended, of course, and for years Mother resented this fact. She resented knowing that there were people who'd pick the pockets of the dead and get away with it. Perhaps that's why we developed an aversion to trips of all kinds and learned to find peace, if not joy, by staying home. Perhaps that's why I fastened the car's seatbelt around the teddy bear. And perhaps that's the reason I was about to make such a car trip, in spite of the government's warning to go outside only for what was considered an essential need. *This* was an essential need.

I closed the back door and sat in the driver's seat. I turned the ignition and opened the map on my phone's GPS. I knew the way, but my hands were trembling, and I feared my thoughts might distract me. I considered making a call, but to whom? All of Mother's friends had passed away. Mine were considered high risk due to their age, and were in quarantine. No one would be able to keep me company, so why even bother? It was the only time I've regretted not keeping in touch with any of the family members of the other victims of the crash. We met a few of them after the accident, but Mother rejected the idea of contacting them again.

"Pain is personal, even if the trauma is shared," she announced, and that was the end of it. As I continued my drive, I wished I had fought back. I wished I had reacted differently. But once Mother had erected a wall between herself and any subject it took all of my energy to break through it, and I was tired of failing. It was easier simply to let her be.

I focused my attention on driving. The road was dry and empty like we had become because Mother willed it so. The lack of traffic in the city shouldn't have surprised me. I had already ventured out for groceries, and all the roads had been deserted then, too. But when I got to the store, things were different. There were people everywhere — lining up, going in, and coming out.

On the highway now, the teddy bear and I drove in total silence and solitude. It felt like the world had ended. And in a way, for me, it had. Did the teddy bear sense it, too?

When I arrived at the retirement home, I saw several signs forbidding entry. I disobeyed each and every one of them. After parking in front of the main entrance, I stepped out of the car to retrieve the teddy. Cradling it like a baby, I walked towards the door. I thought about peeking through a window, but I held myself back. Before my knees had a chance to betray me, I placed the teddy on the ground next to the front door, and returned to the car as fast as I could. At my age it is not advisable to run.

A rock had spontaneously grown inside my throat by the time I dialed the number.

"It's by the door." My voice sounded like a five-year-old's.

"On my way." I recognized the voice that had given me the news a few hours before. I saw the nurse come outside, her face covered by a protective mask, and pick up the teddy bear in her hands. The bright blue of her latex gloves made the plush fur look even more discoloured. She turned towards me and waved goodbye.

"It'll be done as you requested," she yelled before disappearing back inside. I stayed there for a few minutes, unsure of what to do next, trying to slow my breathing, to defog my eyes.

MOTHER WAS NOT included in that night's updated count of victims of a virus that preys on people who are alone and isolated and suffocates them to death. Hers was a generous death, a heart attack while she was sleeping. She would've liked that; she wouldn't have wanted to be part of any such statistic. Numbers didn't mean anything to her, only that which was tangible. That's why I asked for her to be laid to rest with the teddy bear in her arms. Holding a glass of wine in my hand, and still without the energy to share the news with anyone, the only thing that consoled me was the thought of Mother merged with Father in that last hug they had long been denied.

Apartment 91B

THE DESERT AT this time of night seems to lose itself in the sky, like the sea blending into the horizon.

"It's a mute ocean," I told Malena when we first arrived here. "Isn't it pretty?"

"It's a dead ocean," she corrected me before going silent for the rest of the afternoon. The wind blew her hair into her face but she didn't let me pull it back into a ponytail. Perhaps she thought her tousled mane would prevent me from noticing she was crying. She was already mature beyond her years.

I recalled this memory last night as I listened to the wind blowing against my bedroom walls and windows. How strange, how frail the drywall appeared to be during our early days here. I had been an extra in a movie once, and when I first stepped into our apartment I remember thinking that it had been built with the same temporary materials as those sets I thought I had forgotten. I used to share my bed with Malena—her body curled against mine—and couldn't help thinking of the Big Bad Wolf, fearing the wind would tear this place, this apartment made of sticks, to splinters. How hard it was for me to feel secure. Ridiculous, in hindsight, because it didn't mean a thing that our houses and buildings back home were made of bricks. We had been defeated. Devoured. The Big Bad Wolf was real. Who could ever be safe?

"The wind is very strong here so it can push all the bad stuff away," I whispered in Malena's ear one night when even the glass in our windows seemed to tremble with fear. Later, as the weeks, months, and then years passed by, she got used to the fury of the wind, and I stopped worrying about it. Until last night, when it picked up again as if it knew Malena was about to fly back to Florence. It seemed eager to push her away from this place. Away from me.

I had promised Malena that I wouldn't cry and I kept my promise. At the airport, at least. But as soon as I was home, I crumbled. At first I didn't even change her bedsheets. I wanted to keep her scent trapped somewhere, to imagine that I could still cuddle up next to her. But then I realized I couldn't stand seeing her empty closet, the washroom shelf without her perfume. It reminded me of Ernesto's full wardrobe and half-empty bottle of aftershave. I'm bad at dealing with absence. I'm also bad at waiting—always have been. If staying home alone, knowing that she wouldn't return at the end of the day, made the hours feel endless, spending the night indoors would have been unbearable. I had to go out, breathe some fresh air. Face the Wolf.

So here I am. From the edge of Highway I-10, I behold the vastness that extends out from my feet. Miles of sandy soil, shrubs, cacti. The air is crisp. Cars buzz by in the background. I wait until my eyes get accustomed to the dark and wonder how Malena is doing. If everything is the way she imagined before her departure. Was she enjoying the humid summer air?

Once my eyes have adapted, I start walking. I have to do this, so I push myself and stumble against a rock. The pain in my ankle makes me stop, reconsider my own body. I feel old. I'm braving a moonless night. My entire life feels like that: deprived of light. Without a purpose. I had a very clear objective while I cared for Malena. I had made a promise to Ernesto and I fulfilled it. He would've done the same, I have no doubt about it. But would he feel the same if he were in my shoes? Or am I betraying his memory by allowing myself to drift away? Because now that my duty is done, even breathing seems pointless.

• • •

MALENA HAD JUST turned eight when we moved here. Ours was a long and expensive flight made even harder because Malena threw a tantrum. Then she wouldn't talk to me for days after our arrival. I remember cursing Ernesto for putting me in such a position, for leaving me alone. For leaving *us* alone. Without him, we didn't belong in Buenos Aires. I don't know why Malena was so keen on going back to the place where we suffered so much. Why couldn't Florence come here instead? She was the one who had chosen not to accompany us. The one who had insisted on staying put. Florence, with her pointy ears and long fingers, a visage so prematurely aged even then that it's hard for me to imagine her appearance now. Malena didn't take after her at all, except, of course, in her stubborness.

THE WOLF LAUNCHES its first attack against me, and I'm forced to hold my breath, tighten my lips, and close my eyes to protect myself from the sand. There are goosebumps all over my skin. I haven't felt this cold since God-knows-when.

I'm lying. I remember exactly when it was that I felt this cold, this exposed. And God wasn't there.

I continue walking. The soil is uneven, bumpy. I wonder what nocturnal animals are lurking nearby. Scorpions? Snakes? Spiders? None of them are as scary as the ones I've met before, the ones who lock you up and pin you down and enjoy making you scream until you wish you had never been born. Until you beg to die. But they don't kill you, no. Allowing you to live is their poison.

I THINK ABOUT the staircase that leads to Florence's apartment. Number 91B, in bronze — or something that looks like bronze. I picture it in my mind and it's as if I'm there. The hallway smells musty; there must be mould somewhere, underneath the faded wallpaper, perhaps? Apartment 91B is a museum where Florence's entire life is on display. A dry inkwell, daguerreotype photographs, Limoges porcelains, yellowed postcards, and Ernesto's guitar, which has been silent since he was taken prisoner. The silence is good; it's actually *very* good, because any steps echoing on the wooden floor, any voices coming from the other side of the door put me on edge. I need to mute my memories. I choose to focus on the silence because when I hear the voices and the steps approaching, fear turns my whole body into water and I freeze.

I REMEMBER THIS:

Florence hugs my baby girl and defends her in a way that I can't because the men have kicked me in the stomach and cuffed my hands. The last thing I see before they drag me away is my little Malena, sheltered in her grandmother's embrace. They are both crying, their voices blending with those of the men who are arresting me. Men in uniform. I cannot help thinking this is a good sign. I want to reassure Malena and Florence, tell them that I'll come back, see? Because it's the police who are taking me, not men in civilian clothes, driving unmarked cars. But I cannot tell them anything because my voice has been punched out of my body and is now lost. Lost in the same way I myself am about to be lost for five years, four months, and sixteen days. Five years, four months, and sixteen days during which time Florence never brings Malena to visit me. Not even once.

"Seeing you in jail would be too hard for her," Florence said. "She's doing well; she's happy, why upset her balance?"

"Perhaps because not seeing her mother at all will be worse than seeing her in jail."

"You don't want your child to have that image of you, believe me. I'm doing you a favour, dear."

And all those days, weeks, months, and years of seeing my child only in photographs fall upon me with the full weight of their cruelty when I have her before me again, so tall and independent, speaking in full sentences filled with words that I didn't get to teach her. She's playing, walking in Florence's shoes, which are still too big for her, perhaps as big as mine, but I don't get to find that out because she doesn't want to come near me. She doesn't want to touch me. I have a hard time understanding what happened. I barely recognize my own daughter or the apartment, even though everything inside it remains the same.

All I know is this: nothing in Apartment 91B is mine. Only Malena.

I ALSO REMEMBER this:

When I return to Apartment 91B and Florence places a warm cup of tea in my hands, everything looks the same as before except for me. The mirror by the front door spits in my face the traces of five years, four months, and sixteen days. Emotions and experiences I don't have the words to describe. It forces me to notice my damaged teeth; it magnifies my nose, once straight like Malena's but later punched into a hump that now makes me look like a witch. An unfamiliar, ferocious anger boils through my body and erupts like a volcano. The next thing I know, I have thrown the teacup against the mirror, and not only am I cursed with more years of bad luck, but my lanky and distant daughter is staring at me in fear. Her grandmother hugs her and takes her to her bedroom, and I feel like crying but have lost the strength to do even that.

• • •

MALENA'S ABSENCE HAS opened up a well for me to gaze into that other absence in my life: Ernesto. I rub my eyes and squint, trying to make out a path in front of me, trying not to bump against rocks and shrubs. It wasn't supposed to be this way. Ernesto, Malena, and I were supposed to be happy.

Teaching history wasn't supposed to be dangerous. Teaching Russian literature wasn't supposed to be dangerous. But it was. Ernesto warned me the Junta was coming for the academics, but what were we supposed to do? Alter history to suit the official narrative of the Junta? Pretend Marx, Lenin, and Trotsky never existed?

What I'm convinced set Florence against me, was the fact that I was young, reckless, and naive. I refused to give in to fear. I thought that our professional integrity would count for something. We had an ethical duty towards our students. And Ernesto agreed. But only after I had spoken my mind.

Florence could never accept that I was the one who had come back. She never forgave me, I saw it in her eyes. I took away her son, so she took away my daughter. Then I took her back and brought her here, the next move in our sick and twisted chess game. Then she called to say she had had a heart attack and didn't want to die without seeing her granddaughter again. So Malena's back with her. Checkmate. She's won. Yet somehow I still feel I owe

Florence something. I don't know why. After all, Malena and I lost Ernesto, too.

I WAS A prisoner long after I was set free. The father of my child was gone, disappeared, presumably dead. The people I had considered friends avoided me, probably thinking I had done something to deserve my punishment. Florence thought I was being too hard on them. She thought I was the one who should be patient and give them a second chance. Patient? I had lost five years of my life. When I had accepted that Ernesto wouldn't be coming back, taking Malena somewhere safe, somewhere I could rebuild my life and hers, became my mission.

Once I landed a new teaching job in the United States, I asked Florence to come with us, or at least to consider longer visits for Malena's sake, but she refused. She said she'd never set foot in the country that supported the dictatorship that had taken her son away. The country that had turned the Southern Cone into a bloc of military dictatorships that worked against their own citizens. How could I even consider uprooting my daughter and moving *there*?

Her emotional blackmail did not work as she had hoped. Did she truly expect me to raise my only child in the country where I had been illegally jailed and tortured?

She'd never stop waiting for Ernesto, she said, her eyes accusing me of being a traitor. She had to be there when he came back. Everything had to be kept the same, in place for him. But I had to leave. We had to leave. That's why, even though Malena was afraid of me, even though she didn't include me in any of her games or drawings, even though I knew it was going to be difficult, I forced her on that plane. I dragged her from Río de la Plata across the entire continent to build a new life together in the Arizona desert.

I ALLOW MY gaze to search the horizon. Will I run into someone running in the opposite direction? I wish I had brought water, even a gallon, to leave behind, somewhere, anywhere, to be found. To alleviate someone's thirst. How could I not consider the desperate migrants risking their lives, braving the Wolf, crossing an invisible, dangerous border, chasing their dreams of a better life? I too had been lost and thirsty once. I too had fostered that same illusion. Who could've foreseen that all these years later it would've turned out to be a mirage?

FLORENCE TOLD MALENA that Ernesto's belongings remained intact in Apartment 91B. Malena was anxious to touch them, to be back at that place she knew so well as a child. His shirts are there, clean and ironed, his socks rolled into perfect balls; his favourite books and magazines with his scribbling in the margins of their pages; and even the mug he used for his coffee every morning, which Florence never allowed anyone to touch. Florence, with her hair up in a bun, her smell of old eau de cologne and mothballs, hadn't waited in vain. She had just welcomed my daughter into her arms and her timeless existence.

Malena was particularly anxious to hold the music box again, the one that was shaped like a bird cage with two canaries that would swing to the instrumental theme from *Love Story*. I know that Florence didn't let her have it when we left because she wanted it to serve as bait to lure Malena back to her.

I clench my teeth and keep on walking. I cannot hear cars anymore. There's no other sound except the wind. I hear it, I feel it. It cuts through my clothes and scratches my skin.

I WISH MALENA had stayed here, living in the present instead of retracing her steps into the past. I wish the horror story written on my skin had been enough to prevent her from going back there, to keep her by my side. But "Your story is not my story," she told me repeatedly. "I have to go back, Mom."

As I wade deeper into the dark, I picture Malena smiling as she listens to the song trapped in that music box. Will she try to stick her index finger between the bars of the bird-cage to pet the artificial canaries, as she used to do when she was little? Will she realize, as I do now, that we're like those canaries, trapped in our own music boxes, swinging to the tune of our own sadness?

I picture Malena trying on Ernesto's clothes, breathing life back into them. Trying to imagine the size of his body, the touch of his arms.

She will never know about the times we made love on the living room sofa while Florence was out shopping and Malena was napping in our bedroom.

She will never know the sound of her father's laughter. She will never know how I wished my body were a seashell and his voice the ocean forever kept alive inside me.

She will never know the song he wrote especially for me. The last song he played on the guitar that's hanging from the wall in Apartment 91B.

But she will be happy to try on Florence's shoes and discover they fit a bit tight now. They'll surely laugh together, remembering how big they felt the last time she wore them.

I HAVE FULFILLED my promise to Ernesto, and now I am finally free. But this time around, my freedom serves no purpose. What if Florence convinces Malena to stay, to join her in her quest to find Ernesto's remains? What if she decides to be a part of the demonstrations in which Florence and other mothers, now grandmothers, clamour for justice? A justice that ebbs more than it flows. A justice that is always unjust.

I wonder if Malena will miss me.

I stare down at my hands. Empty. No one to hold on to. Without Malena I lack all courage.

TONIGHT, THERE ARE no stars in the sky. Other than the wind blowing, there is no sound, and for that I am thankful. Silence is the one thing I don't fear.

I can feel the rocks under my feet, my mouth is dry, and I'm shivering. But I force myself to keep going. I must keep going because, unlike Malena, I have nothing—I have nowhere—to return to.

Old Wounds

THIRTY YEARS. I wonder what he looks like now, as a thirty-year-old man. Is he married? Where does he live? Is he happy? I wonder, too, what you look like now, as a forty-seven-year-old woman. Are *you* happy? We were eighteen the last time we were together. I still see a bit of the teenager I used to be when I look at myself in the mirror. Not because of my looks, no, nothing like that. I've aged — haven't we all? Seeing your clothes straining at the seams and colouring your own hair while isolating alone in the middle of a pandemic is enough to kill off any remaining delusions of youth. No. I see that teenager peeping out every time I doubt myself, or when I want to drown my sorrows in tequila. Or when tomorrow's anniversary draws near. They say some things never change. How have *you* changed?

I guess I could call you. If I really wanted to, I mean. I know people who could probably give me your number. Or your email address, if I really wanted to reach out. What would you say? Would you be happy to hear from me? Or annoyed? Surprised, for sure. Would we make small talk? Or lapse into an uncomfortable silence? Don't worry. I won't call or email you. It's just that I've been alone for eighty-five days and counting, out only once a week to buy groceries (food is so expensive here! Is it expensive where you live, too? Do you complain about that as well? One day you're young, and the next you're complaining about the price of groceries. Is there a meme for this?). I've had Zoom meetings and phone calls and walks and snowfalls and ice storms and rainfalls and rainbows and somehow this quarantine, which by now should be called eightytine or centennialtine, seems longer than the thirty years we haven't talked. And today I need to talk to you. So I will, and you'll listen.

Perhaps it was foolish of me, but I expected you to show up at the funeral home when my mother passed away last year. You could have come, you know? Life was normal back then and her obituary appeared in the newspaper that I know you read. The one that your family used to read, anyway. I'm sure someone must have told you that she died, and that I was in town for her wake and burial. I flew in — worst flight of my life, believe me — to face a casket. I wasn't brave enough to look at my mother's face.

I wanted to remember her the way she was when she was alive. Remember how stylish, how good-looking she was? Why didn't you come to pay your respects? I waited for you. Even while I was deep in the fog of grief, I played different scenarios in my mind. You, entering the room where her casket sat surrounded by nauseating flowers—*Flores para los muertos*; remember we read that book together?—and me, pretending I didn't see you. Or accepting your condolences with indifference. Or breaking down and hugging you. Or calling security to escort you out. You never know how you'll react under stress. Or while you're hurting. But you didn't give me the chance to find out. You didn't even email me. And yes, you *too* could've reached out. You know people who could have put you in touch with me. But you didn't, did you? Not even when my mother was dead, and I had travelled from miles away to put her to rest.

I always thought that being incarcerated was too lenient a punishment for criminals: freaking bastards eat and sleep and shit and breathe for free—on *our* dime—while we kill ourselves working. But now that I've been cooped up with nowhere to go, I've discovered that being locked up is not the real punishment. No. The real punishment is having time to think. To count your mistakes. Your mind spinning over matters like a frantic hamster on its wheel, only to discover—when you stop to catch your breath—that you haven't moved. Thirty years, and here I am. Still eighteen.

You were there then—for my birthday, I mean—and I didn't notice anything out of the ordinary. It doesn't show in the photos, either. You were quiet, that I remember, but I assumed it was because it wasn't your usual crowd, even though Rupert came along. We had already started to drift apart but it was impossible then to foresee how irrevocably. You were wearing a red sweater with shoulder pads—they were all the rage that year—and jeans. I was wearing a shirt that exposed my midriff. April is the cruellest month only if you happen to live on the northern or southern edges of the continent. Our April's warm breath and welcoming arms brought the gift of endless sunshine, so much sunshine it was hard to believe its radiance didn't blind every corner of the world. Why were you wearing a sweater in the middle of April? I should've paid attention, asked you questions, watched you more closely. There's no use chastising myself over it now, yet I do. I was eighteen and it was my party, but I should've been paying attention.

Three-and-a-half months later, the phone rang as I was packing for the trip I had been longing for: six months abroad to celebrate the end of high school, the beginning of real life. I hadn't talked to you much about it because our phone conversations had become infrequent and brief, and I didn't want to rub it in. Instead, I reminisced about how we used to travel together before your father disappeared. No. Allow me to rephrase that. He didn't disappear. That word is reserved for those people who had no intention of leaving. Your father chose to leave. He abandoned you and your mother, my "Auntie," even though she wasn't my aunt. He abandoned you but he abandoned me too, because back in those days my parents were going through a divorce and there was so much yelling and fighting and other things I don't want to remember that your home was my refuge. And your father was the man I looked up to. He abandoned *us*. Except I still *had* my father. And six years later I was getting ready for the trip of a lifetime, thinking about everything and everyone except you. Would you believe me if I told you I still feel guilty about that? After all the years that we were best friends, all the sleepovers, the long hours talking on the phone, the shared dreams. We played Barbies and danced to *Grease* and watched *Friday the 13th* and *Psycho* huddled together. We went shopping and camping (I still feel sorry for the cow that ate your soap when we were washing our hands in the river), and you promised I'd be godmother to your first child and I promised you'd be godmother to mine, and we shared books and games, and then your father left and things changed and you and I changed and then the phone rang.

"We need a favour." It was Rupert.

I was in the midst of folding some clothes, and the phone had a short cord so I couldn't walk freely around the room. I stopped what I was doing, ready to listen. Rupert and I had sat together in grade nine, and I saw him draw terribly pornographic figures all over his notebooks and even on the desk we shared. Women penetrated with humongous penises from behind. Eating the penises. Legs spread open, obscene lines imitating movements. Pubic hair. Why didn't the teachers do something about it? Did they even care?

"Sure." I tried to sound friendly.

"Lisa isn't feeling well. I'm taking her to the doctor, but we don't want her mom to worry so we're going to tell her that Lisa is with you."

Auntie would worry for sure if she heard Lisa wasn't feeling well, but she wouldn't have been able to do much even if she wanted to. She was at work and always stayed late. After your father left, she had to earn a living to support you both. She was always tired, absent, busy, or in a rush. I would gladly save Auntie a worry, especially if it was a worry she didn't need. Mistake number one.

"What's going on?" I asked. I wanted to make sure covering for you was the best decision.

"Bad stomach ache."

I didn't inquire further. I knew you liked to drink. I assumed you had a bad hangover or perhaps you had eaten bad tacos on your way out of the bar. I shouldn't have assumed anything. Mistake number two.

"Okay. But let me know what the doctor says."

We hung up, and I went back to packing. I was listening

to the radio and quickly forgot about the call, until the phone rang again.

"I need you to come with me." Rupert's voice was offhand. As if he had just given me the time.

"What do you mean, come with you?"

"I'll come and get you."

My trip was only two days away, and I had so much left to do. It was impossible.

"What did the doctor say?"

"She'll be fine, but we just found out that Lisa's mom is going to have dinner with your mom at your place. You can't be there. Be ready in ten."

Dinner? Was it already so late? I had to leave because your mother was going to have dinner with my mother and we had lied saying you were with me and not at the doctor's and I never liked lies but for you I agreed to lie. And you couldn't even come to pay your respects at my mother's wake. My mother, who was a friend of your mother's. Of your mother, who said she loved my mother like a sister.

After fixing my hair in a hurry, I grabbed my purse and simply told my mom I was going out for a bite with you ("but your Auntie is coming, why don't you both stay here with us!") and my hands were sweating because I didn't like lying but we were lucky she didn't notice. Rupert was already parked outside. Alone.

"Where's Lisa?"

• • •

DO YOU REMEMBER the trip we took together, back before your father left and my parents were still together, and our mothers took us along for a girls-only week? They bought us identical dolls to match our identical raincoats and identical shoes. Our hotel room was on the third floor, with a view of a nice backyard. My mother had gone out to get us food; you were hungry and you lost your temper and, in the middle of a tantrum, you threw your doll out the window. I remember watching the doll, the brand-new, beautiful baby doll, fall and land face-down on the grass. If she'd been a child, she would've been dead. I remember thinking that. I expected Auntie to rush downstairs to pick up the wounded doll, but instead she pulled you over and hit you until your arms and your face were red, and you were crying and I had never seen Auntie angry like that, so I stood where I was, watching, until she took you in her arms, and you were saying that your arms and your cheeks hurt and Auntie hugged you and kissed you and said I'm sorry I'm sorry I'm sorry and carried you in her arms as if you were a baby and you let her and she held you tight and I envied you because my mother had never hugged me like that.

I ran downstairs to pick up the doll from the grass. She was a bit dirty and dishevelled but I fixed her hair, cleaned her face, and gave her back to you, remember? But you still didn't want her. So I gave you mine and kept yours. I was happy to. I wouldn't have been able to articulate it back then, but now I think that I needed that doll because I understood how she felt. We were meant for each other.

We had already exchanged dolls and calmed down when my mother came back with a special treat: McDonald's. When we sat down to eat, I placed my newly adopted doll on my lap. Your eyes were red from crying. Auntie pretended everything was fine and tried to keep up a cheerful conversation, and my mother didn't notice a thing. Looking back now, forty years later or so, what happened to us at eighteen doesn't seem so surprising.

"WHERE'S LISA?" I expected you to be in the car.

"At the hospital."

My heart skipped a beat. This wasn't the plan. You were supposed to see a doctor and then go back home and be perfectly fine. "What were you doing at the hospital?"

"Stomach ache got worse."

I asked what you'd eaten the day before, if you'd been drinking and how much. I needed to know the kind of pain you were in. "Describe it to me, Rupert." He couldn't say, didn't know how.

The nurse refused to share any information on your condition unless I declared myself your relative and signed the required paperwork. The forms were long and confusing, so I signed them without reading. I needed to know what was going on. Mistake number three. Rupert was standing behind me. There were people around us, waiting. I sat down to wait, too. It was late and I was hungry. What was I going to say when I came back home, starving, after saying that I was having a meal with you? How was I going to hide the fact that you were at the hospital?

Finally, someone called my name. I stood up, trying to appear mature and in control. A nurse approached and handed me a bag with your clothes inside: a sweater, jeans, underwear, black shoes. Then she placed in my hand your earrings and that gold chain you always wore around your neck. I held my breath. Why was I receiving all your things like this?

"She's doing great." The nurse smiled.

"Can I see her?" I asked, trying not to sound like the absolute idiot I felt like.

"Sure! Once the baby's born."

I froze. Had I heard that correctly? I turned to Rupert, livid. I would've punched him if my hands had been free. A baby? All this time you were pregnant and I didn't know. My mother and I didn't know. Did Auntie know? I dashed out into the street. I needed to yell, and I couldn't do so in the waiting room. Rupert followed me.

"Why didn't you tell me?"

I was pacing up and down on the sidewalk. Rupert's face was blank.

"Lisa didn't want anyone to know."

"Anyone? So no one knew? How can you hide a pregnancy?"

"She bound herself."

I couldn't hold back my tears. You bound yourself? How could you do that to your own child? And to yourself? Why didn't you ask for help? Why didn't you tell anyone?

"And what are you going to do?"

"Whatever Lisa wants." Rupert avoided my eyes. It was probably for the best. I had never liked him much. How could you do those things—those obscene things he had drawn in his notebook and on our school desk—with him? Why didn't you protect yourself? It wasn't like we didn't know about condoms. You and I were sitting together at school when the teacher took out the banana and we had that lesson. Remember how hard we laughed?

"And what does she want?"

"Doesn't want it."

I had to pause. Inhale. Exhale.

"So what are you going to do?"

"That's why we called you." Rupert turned his back to me.

• • •

IT WAS ALREADY late, and I had to find a pay phone to call my mother and tell her when I'd be back. I told another lie, said we had run into some friends, decided to catch a movie. Mistake number four. There were too many mistakes that day, but he was not one of them: your baby boy, weighing barely four pounds but otherwise healthy. A miracle. He needed a home, and it was my duty to find one. It was what you wanted from me, remember? Then why did you and Rupert tell our schoolmates, later on, that I had taken your child away? As if I went around stealing people's babies? When at a school reunion someone brought it up, I could hardly believe my ears. I had to tell them my side of the story, and I broke down because I had never spoken about it and I got emotional and the entire reunion was ruined and I know they gossiped about us, and that was your fault. Not mine. Because I didn't tell anyone. You did. You. The one who didn't want anyone to find out.

When I went upstairs to see you—I, not Rupert, the cowardly piece of shit—you were sitting up in that bed, staring at your fingernails. You always took such great care of your nails. Mine looked like Smarties no matter what I did, but yours were elegant, and you were almost in a trance staring at them, so much so that you barely looked up when I stood next to you. I don't know if you remember the conversation we had, but I do. I told you that if you wanted me to find a home for your child I would do so.

I knew people, people who didn't know you and who loved babies and would be happy to adopt a newborn, and no one else needed to know if that's what you wished, but perhaps you should think about it a bit harder, it was your child, and Auntie would be mad at you at the beginning but then she'd forgive you, it was her grandchild. And Rupert was a motherfucker, but this was also his parents' grandchild. The baby had a family.

"I don't want him." Your words. Not mine.

IT WOULD'VE ALL worked out if you hadn't blown it. Why did you give the hospital your phone number instead of mine? Did you secretly want Auntie to find out and stop you? We were both equally wrong about her, I guess.

"You were in it all along," Auntie said to me, her jaws clenched. "You liar."

There was no way to convince her that I had only found out the night before.

"You signed papers? What did they say?" My mother was furious. I shrugged. How would I know what they said? "If something had happened to her while giving birth, you would've been liable, did you know that?"

I shook my head.

No.

I was only thinking about the baby.

The baby needed a home. What was going to happen to the baby? Did Rupert's parents know?

No.

No one was to know.

The baby would be sent to an orphanage. Auntie didn't want anyone that we knew to adopt him. Her daughter wouldn't bring such dishonour to her family, she said. Any possibility of contact in the future had to be prevented.

Horrified, I stormed out of the hospital, where we had been giving everyone present the show of a lifetime.

My mother saved the day, did you know that? Or perhaps you never found out. It was her idea to call our pediatrician and ask him to intervene, find a good family for the baby, someone we didn't know. I drove you home from the hospital the next day so no one would see you arrive with Rupert after being away overnight. We hardly spoke during the drive. You were in the back seat and I was driving so slowly, so carefully, because you had just given birth and I assumed you'd still be in pain. I didn't want to hurt you. And we were silent, and when I tried to find your eyes in the mirror, you avoided me.

My mother, to whose wake you didn't bother to come, drove your newborn son, in the company of your mother, to the pediatrician's office, so that his new parents — a young couple who cried tears of joy, the doctor said — could collect him. Yes, it was illegal and we all risked going to jail for you and I would still do it again. Would you?

There's something about this pandemic that's flooded me with memories. And I've been haunted by this chapter in our lives, the last one of our friendship. My trip that summer was bittersweet. I cried whenever I thought about you. You were pregnant and nobody noticed. Did no one hug you? There were boys during that trip that wanted to go out with me, make out with me, but I couldn't stand the thought of being close to any man. And I wrote you letters but didn't have the courage to put them in the mail.

The last image I have is of you struggling to get out of my car. We didn't even say goodbye.

Perhaps it's because tomorrow will be your son's thirtieth birthday.

Every year around this date I think of you. Of him. This is a milestone, however: three decades have gone by. Why do all those days—months, years—feel shorter than the time I've been cooped up now, in isolation? Why was I even hoping you'd come to see me or reach out to me when my mother passed away?

Fresh wounds open old wounds, I guess.

Rear-View Mirror

I FIX MY eyes on the road to focus my mind. All that packing and arguing made us late and night is about to fall. Abby
is in the back seat, wearing her earphones and a frown.
She's seventeen but if she keeps on glowering this way, she
will soon develop the same wrinkle as Father, a crease that
could have been carved with a sickle. You can take the X out
of the Y and yadda yadda yadda. Out of all the memories
I have of Mother, I'd like to delete that one in particular, her
voice saying "you can take the X out of the Y . . ." because it's
loaded with a curse, an inescapable omen. Karma. I know
full well that, were she still alive, she'd say that I had it all
coming, that I deserve it because I was the worst child.
That because I made her suffer so much, it's now my turn
to suffer even more — words she would never have said to
my brother, of course, because it's only women who have

to be tough and take it all in stride. But no more, Mother. Look at me. No more.

This toll highway, newly paved, looks deceptively like it follows a straight line, but it doesn't. I know that we're about to hit the curves, and the landscape and vegetation will start to change. Right now, it's still dry and barren around us, but as we approach the ocean everything will become green and lush, the breeze salty. I haven't been here since that trip I took with Mario, when we made love on the sand—he, so very excited, his erection lasting forever while I felt so very uncomfortable yet obliged to feign ecstasy. I don't know why back then everything seemed "so very," but I do know I was "so very" stupid. That was the trip that planted Abby on the map—and embedded her in my body, my arms, my life, in the air I breathe, around my neck, and across my throat.

"Could you at least turn up the air conditioning? I can barely feel it back here. It's like you want me to melt in this fucking car."

I turn up the air conditioning to the max. The noise it makes is irritating but it's better than listening to Abby complain. I clench my teeth and take a deep breath. I've given up asking her to stop talking to me like this. It's useless. Choose your battles, they say. I've decided not to put up a fight on this particular front anymore.

Trying to numb my mind, I force myself to focus on the road, but I immediately start thinking about Medea. I've been thinking about Medea for quite a few days, actually. About Medea, Oedipus, Clytemnestra, and the Greeks who, thousands of years ago, already knew everything that needed to be known about life.

But especially about Medea. Medea, who betrayed her own noble father to help Jason steal the Golden Fleece for Corinth. Medea, who fathered Jason's children only to be banished so that he could marry the King of Corinth's daughter, Glauce, a woman much younger than Medea, with an impeccable body, the body of a woman who hadn't borne any children. Horrible. Unthinkable.

So why shouldn't Medea have avenged this betrayal with blood? It was only natural that she poisoned Glauce and her royal father, that Corinthian king. And Jason? Why should he have any descendents? Why should he have the children he said he loved but didn't hesitate to abandon? Of course, it's Medea who's despised for killing her own children. But who gets angry at Jason? Who tells him that he is a traitor, a colossal son of a bitch, a full-on bastard?

I tried to read Greek mythology with Abby once, but she wasn't interested. She's never enjoyed reading. "She gets that from your mother-in-law," Mother said. "I raised you to be a cultured person, unlike that you-know-what husband of yours." And now Abby. YouTube, Snapchat, Instagram, and TikTok are the temples at which Abby worships. If she had to choose between having no internet ever again or becoming an orphan, I'd no longer be alive. Right now there's no Wi-Fi, so she's listening to music she has stored on her phone, and I can feel her contempt drilling through the back of my skull. If she could shoot laser beams through her eyes, I'd have been decapitated long ago. Thank God teenagers have no superpowers; if they did, we'd be way more fucked up than we already are, especially now, in the midst of this family crisis and a pandemic. Oedipus was made a hero for eradicating the plague in Thebes, without anyone knowing that he had caused it in the first place by killing his father and marrying his mother. He even had four children with her. Four children. I only have one, so I can understand Oedipus only partially, but the person I fully understand is his father, who ordered him killed as an infant to prevent the fulfillment of the prophecy that said his own son would become his murderer.

"Did you pack anything to eat?" Abby takes out one of her earphones and lets it drop over her chest. Drums can be heard torturing the tiny speaker. "I bet you didn't, am I right?" I straighten my arm and, without taking my eyes off the road, pass her my purse.

"There are cookies in there."

Abby yanks the purse out of my hand and throws it next to her on the back seat.

"I'm no longer five, in case you haven't noticed." She seeks my gaze in the rear-view mirror, defiant. I'd like to tell her that of course I've noticed she's no longer five: she used to be adorable when she was that age. "Your cookies are disgusting. What about my vegan ones? I bet you forgot them."

Her words sting like a whip. I had to remember to bring *her* vegan cookies? I'd like to tell her that, yes, on top of packing her medication, my clothes, our most important documents — among them the title to our house, which by sheer luck I happened to have — that on top of getting a divorce in the midst of a global pandemic because that's precisely what it took, a pandemic, for the idiot that I am, the fucking idiot that I've been all this time, to realize that her father had been cheating on me for years, that Abby has siblings whose existence she knows nothing about, that I don't even know if my marriage is legal anymore because the other woman, too, claims to be his wife; that on top of all this, and the haste with which we left so I wouldn't have to face her fucking father for the rest of the fucking quarantine; yes, of course I forgot to pack her cookies, which, by the way, taste like sawdust.

"I guess I was in such a hurry that I forgot. I thought you had them. I'm sorry."

"You thought *I* had them? I didn't even want to leave to begin with."

No, neither did I. I didn't want to leave the only place I'd called home for years in a hurry, as if I was the one who was at fault. But if we had stayed, the bomb would have exploded in Abby's face. It's one thing to digest your parents' divorce at seventeen; it's a whole different thing to discover, when you're going through a depression, that your father is a liar who leads a double life. I need distance so I can think, so I can decide how to proceed, how to protect myself and, most importantly, how to protect Abby.

"I wish I'd died."

I feel like screaming, but I clench my teeth and squeeze the wheel like I'm trying to strangle it. The darkness that is slowly enveloping us reminds me that it's time to turn on my headlights.

"Don't you ever dare say that to me again." But my tongue spits out the words like bullets and that's the opposite of what I intended. No, I don't mean to upset her. "I'm sorry. I apologize. That came out wrong. Forgive me. Must be exhaustion." And fear, I should've added, but I keep that to myself and exhale loudly instead.

Abby's jaw is tense. She reminds me so much of her father and of myself at that age. But I never had a boyfriend die in a car accident, I was never diagnosed with depresssion — although after Abby was born, I'm certain I had something close to it. They gave it the cutesy name of "baby blues," but they weren't cute. Every single day in the shower I'd burst out sobbing, asking myself what the hell I had done with my life. But little by little the feeling of despair subsided and I forgot all about it until Abby was diagnosed—and never, under any circumstance, would I have considered becoming vegan.

It was all because of Louis and his love of cows. It was Louis who told us that cows, like elephants, are capable of forming complex social groups and establishing deep relationships. They are capable of holding memories over a long period of time, and grudges against other cows if they feel they have been mistreated. Who would have thought that a cow could ever mistreat another cow? How does that go? Do they kick one another? Do they give each other the side-eye? No, Abby said. Eyes with such long, gorgeous lashes are incapable of giving anyone a mean look.

"Cows," insisted Louis, "remember the experiences they have been through." They remember that their newborn calves have been snatched from them, bawling in despair and fear, only to be cut into little pieces to be displayed and sold on sterile styrofoam trays for humans to enjoy while they, their heartbroken mothers, remain permanently incarcerated, their generous udders feeding endless plastic snakes that never stop sucking the life from them. Cows can give milk for up to ten months a year, then they are given a two-month break to be impregnated again and give birth to yet another calf that will also be dragged away.

A while ago I read somewhere, I don't remember exactly where, that during the days of slavery in the United States,

Black women were forced to be wet nurses to the children of their white masters while their own little ones withered away in front of the women's very eyes. That's an image that has been making the rounds in my head as well: dark-skinned breasts full of milk that white owners would squeeze out by force using their bare hands. How that must have hurt and enraged those helpless women I cannot even imagine. Up until your newborn child's mouth latches onto your breast for the first time, it's impossible to realize how painful engorged breasts, plugged milk ducts, or cracked nipples oozing blood can be. Abby, of course, knows nothing of this.

"Don't talk like that, Abby. You're the best thing I have." The crack in my voice makes me fear the dam inside me will break, but I manage to contain it.

"You'd be better off without me. Even your divorce would be easier if I wasn't around."

All those times she was a baby and used to cry and I had no idea how to calm her down, all those nights I wished I could rewind my life and erase Mario and Abby the way you used to erase images from a videotape, rewind my life so I could be young again but less stupid and never have sex on the beach, much less sex without a condom. I remember how all that desperation accumulated like burning steam inside my chest, becoming something else, something entirely different that I could not give a name to when I found her unconscious in her room and I thought I'd lost her forever. It had been weeks since Louis's accident, weeks during which Abby couldn't eat or sleep. Weeks when she cried incessantly at night, just like when she was a baby. Weeks when I didn't know how to help, how to console her. Mario had insisted that I give her time, give her space, up until that awful daybreak. The terror of losing her is a tide that never falls. It only rises.

"My life would make no sense without you," I tell her. And I mean it. It's one thing for children to grow up and leave home, and another entirely to lose them forever. How can anyone learn to live with that void?

"Nothing makes sense, Mom. We're in the middle of a pandemic, people are dying by the thousands, there are no jobs, I can't go see my friends, we've been cooped up for months, and it will probably be a couple of years before people can even travel again. My generation is totally fucked. There's no future. And now, on top of all that, this quarantine has made you and Dad hate each other so much that you're getting a divorce. I wish I had been in that car with Louis. I really do."

"Don't. Please," I try to say it gently even though I feel like spewing out everything I've kept to myself: that I wish she hadn't met stupid Louis at all, that I wish her father hadn't turned out to be a jerk and we hadn't discovered it so soon after Louis' accident, that I wish I knew how to mend her broken heart, that I know she is not herself when she says those things — that the snake rearing its head through her mouth is becoming more real and more terrifying every day. But I keep quiet; we're entering a curve. The sinuous part of the highway has emerged. We start heading down now. The vegetation is lush and abundant, dark green. I wish I knew the names of the trees out here so I could distract Abby by commenting on them. I know that the air outside is warm and humid, that it has a salty smell, and I regret choosing this destination. I should've chosen a place that I had never been to before, a place that held no memories. "It's not that your father and I hate each other because of the quarantine, Abby. You know that he has another woman."

"Yes, but he apologized to you. He apologized to you and he was crying and you wouldn't forgive him."

"Would you like me to forgive him just like that time when he hit me?" I wish I could take my words back the second I see Abby's eyes well up. Why did I have to remind her of that? I'm so stupid! "This is different, Abby. Infidelity is different."

"But it's you he cares about!"

Oh, the innocence! If he cared about me he wouldn't be a bigamist. And he wouldn't have fathered other children. Was that his revenge? He didn't answer when I asked him, but I'm positive it was. I think it was his revenge because

I got pregnant after Abby but kept it a secret from him and chose not to have that baby. It would have all been perfect had it not been for the hemorrhage. "God punishes women who do what you did," Mother told me. "How dare you deny Abby the wonderful opportunity of having a little brother?" Those were the exact words I needed to hear to convince me I never wanted to see her or my brother ever again.

But all I said was, "Betrayal shouldn't be forgiven, Abby. I hope that you never choose to remain by the side of a man who betrays you."

"He's my dad!"

I decide it's best not to say anything else to my little Electra. I feel a huge empathy for Clytemnestra. All the bullshit she had to endure from Agamemnon, and on top of that her daughter hated her instead of him, the traitor, the unfaithful one, the one who picked Iphigenia, his favourite, to sacrifice before the war, instead of Electra. Not Electra. How will Abby react when she finds out the whole truth? Will she still be defending Mario in spite of the forged documents, the lies, the hidden step-siblings? Is there an Iphigenia?

The curves become steeper, sharper, and more frequent. There are not many cars on the highway, but several trucks have passed us. Truck drivers know the road well; they go over the speed limit. I don't like doing that. I'm careful. I watch out for animals or people crossing the road unexpectedly — I know that behind the lush palm trees and bushes, villages have sprouted and grown. I'm alert. Eighteen years of marriage. Almost a lifetime! A cow's lifetime, at least. I remember Louis saying that cows can live up to twenty-two years, which means that they lose — no, they don't lose, they are robbed of — around a dozen calves throughout their lifetime. Do cows give their calves names?

A cow and her calf were crossing the highway in front of Louis. He swerved to avoid running them over and his car fell twelve metres down a cliff. Twelve meters into the void. I don't like to think about the fall, yet I do. I think about the noise — glass breaking, airbags deploying, metal hitting rocks and bushes — the world spinning out of control, the pain, the taste of blood, the silence. The unbearable silence.

The cow — we learned about this later — had managed to escape a nearby farm and was trying to save its baby. Louis helped her save it. That's what Louis's parents told us. They were crying, yet they seemed so proud. Proud that their son had given his life to save a cow and her calf? And Abby? Who will give their life to save Abby?

I look in the rear-view mirror and see that she's sleeping. Thank goodness. That will make the next bit less difficult. I step on the gas pedal.

The Other Side

ON HER KNEES and facing the concrete wall, Magda
doesn't know what to do with her hands. She covers her
ears to muffle the cries, but her arms are tired and she's not
strong enough to hold the position. They want her to stay
erect, won't even let her rest on her heels. Hugging herself,
rubbing her arms to fight the cold seems as futile as trying
to light a fire with damp wood. The cold has travelled deep
under her skin and wrapped itself around her bones. Like
a plaster cast, it impedes her movements, slows her down.
Her nipples are on the offensive, showing through her bra
and T-shirt, and she hates them. She hates them because
that's all the guards stare at when they speak to her, never
lifting their eyes. She wishes she could replace her body
with the one she had had when Daddy left and she was flat
and skinny and ignorant of the secrets of the world. She

wishes she could get rid of her breasts and the cries and especially the cold. If only she could rest her weight on her heels for a few minutes! But out of the corner of her eye she can still see the olive-green dress shirt and slacks, the blue stripe running the length of the seam down to the black boots. If she allows herself to relax again, she is sure the baton will not stop at the chicken-wire fence.

Magda remembers the huge jackhammer that broke apart the sidewalk back home, and it occurs to her that all the concrete in the world has decided to seek revenge here in this detention centre, against their helpless bodies, prodding flesh and joints. The discomfort she was already feeling in her lower back when she arrived has become a stabbing pain that makes her long to curl up into a ball. But of course that would be small comfort — cold is even harder to tolerate when lying on the bare concrete floor. She remembers watching a documentary with Doña Toñita, her neighbour, about concentration camps. The bald heads peeking out from what looked like bunk beds in the barracks had haunted her for several days. Then she stopped thinking about it. Until now. Because it is only now that she realizes those prisoners had beds, while people here don't. There are not even enough metal-foil blankets for them all. How did people ever come up with the idea, she wonders, that hell's punishment is its heat, when true hell must surely resemble this place, with its walls and floor like slabs of ice; the deafening, ceaseless crying; the smell of soiled diapers and dirt and sweat; the fluorescent white light cutting through closed eyelids without a break. Never has Magda yearned so much for darkness — for silence — before.

Although she has only known him for two days — and under different circumstances she would have found this impossible to believe — Magda can tell which cries are Juan Carlitos's. What can only be described as a distinctive, almost rhythmic pattern to his sobbing prompted one of the guards to make fun of him. His words, as well as the laughter they elicited, are etched inside her head: "This one's a singer. I think we have a full orchestra here. All we're missing is a conductor!" If Juan Carlitos's mother had known, if Magda herself had known how things would turn out, perhaps things would be different. But *el hubiera no existe*, there's no point in wasting time on wouldhavebeens. Too late for that now.

Magda had walked — for how many days? — only because she was convinced everything would be better once she crossed the border. Doña Toñita had told her that all she needed to do was tell the guards she had come looking for her daddy.

"They sure don't like us," she had said, "but there's some kind of rule that says they must help the children, and not even their new president can go against that. I heard it on the news." Doña Toñita was always watching the news or documentaries, and sometimes when her mother left her home alone, Magda was invited over and sat in front of the television next to her.

Once Magda had made it across the border, Doña Toñita said, the guards would help her get to her daddy. They would help her make the phone call, and he would be surprised but elated to hear her voice after all this time, and then he would come pick her up and bring her to live with him as he had promised. Magda had played the scene over in her mind again and again. The tall, blond border guard (So handsome! Just like on television!) would offer her a nice glass of cold, white, creamy American milk, perhaps even some home-made cookies, and smile at her while he dialed the number that she had memorized but had never been allowed to call from home. This was all she was thinking about when the boy's mother approached her. The sun was shining and the air was so hot that Magda's T-shirt was sticking to her skin, her mouth dry and sticky, her feet swollen in her flip-flops and blackened with dirt. She remembers how relieved, how happy she felt to have arrived. There was no breeze. Magda remembers the two flags hanging limp from the posts, but she didn't understand that they were sending a message: this is not where new lives begin.

Magda had stopped to stare at the long lineup of cars waiting to cross the border. So many people in so many different cars waiting patiently for their turn. In traffic like this, Magda thought, drivers usually honk their horns or try desperately to switch lanes. Here, they all waited with their windows up, enjoying the air conditioning, indifferent to the vendors offering all sorts of merchandise: giant crucifixes, hand-embroidered placemats, cold soft drinks, peanuts and chips and chewing gum. (To think that she had longed for air conditioning!) There was a faint smell of gasoline and dust. Certain that she would never miss what was being left behind, Magda was about to make her way across the bridge when Juan Carlitos's mother reached out for her arm and stopped her. She was crying.

"Excuse me?" The woman's accent betrayed her as a foreigner. Magda immediately knew she was not Mexican, but from somewhere in Central America. She knew there were hundreds of Central Americans, if not thousands, trying to make their way to the United States through Mexico, but she had never actually met one. "Are you crossing to the other side?"

Crossing to the other side. The other side of what? But Magda didn't know then what she knows now, and was not able to question the woman's choice of words. Her words were the same ones used by everybody, the same words she had heard Daddy repeat over and over as she was growing up: *Cruzar pa'l otro lado. El Otro Lado*: the Other Side, meaning the good side, the better side; as opposed to This Side, where poverty, corruption, and violence rules and dreams are born dead.

"Yes." Magda fixed her eyes in the woman's hair. She had dyed it blond but her black roots had grown in, looking like the feathers of an exotic bird, black and yellow with hints of grey. She had a black eye. Her lids were red and swollen.

"Can you please help my son get across?"

It took Magda a few moments to grasp what she meant.

"Help him get across?" Only then did she notice the child. He could not be more than four years old. He was dressed in a T-shirt, shorts, and running shoes. "How come you aren't taking him yourself?"

"I must find my daughter. But I need to make sure he's safe first." Her pleading expression disarmed Magda. She should have asked more questions, but all she could think of was how different this woman was from her own mother. She didn't know where the woman's daughter was or what had happened to her, but she envied her. The woman went on: "My sister lives in Texas; she's waiting for him." She showed Magda the orange notecard with a name and address written in black marker that she had attached to the boy's T-shirt with a safety pin. Then she crouched and gave him one last kiss and hug.

"Go with her, my love," she instructed him. "This kind lady will take you to your aunt's. I'll be there really soon, I promise." Magda felt the urge to correct the woman: she was not a "lady," she was just fourteen. But there was no time. The woman gave them a gentle push and waved goodbye as both children began walking across the bridge. Juan Carlitos was wailing all the while, and it seems to Magda that he has not stopped since.

SOME OF THE other girls in the Doghouse—that's what the guards called the first place where they were taken after they had crossed the bridge—thought that Juan Carlitos was Magda's son. Crying like a wounded puppy, the boy followed her every movement. How lucky they were to have been allowed to stay together, those girls said. Magda was so tired, so sleepy, that she had dozed off in a corner before she could explain that she and Juan Carlitos were not even related. Sobbing quietly, the boy sat next to her until a guard kicked Magda's leg and yelled at her to wake up. As she was rising to her feet, she decided to see if this new guard would be more willing to hear her out and help them.

"Did you call my daddy? I gave the other guard his number."

The guard shook his head no and told her to join the others as they lined up to leave the room.

"Did you call the boy's aunt? Her number was written on the card he had pinned to his T-shirt. Did you reach her?"

But the guard told her curtly to be quiet and keep walking. She was thirsty and hungry but no one had offered her anything to eat or drink. Perhaps she could ask to use the washroom and drink some tap water? She was longing to wash her hands and face. They told her she had to wait until they arrived at the new location. Magda felt hopeful. Leaving a place that was nicknamed the Doghouse could only be good. But her hope faded as soon as she found herself surrounded by chicken-wire fencing in the next place, which was so aptly dubbed the Freezer.

ON HER KNEES and facing the wall, Magda wishes she could be a dog, a dog in a doghouse instead of a girl locked up in this chilly chicken coop. Except, she thinks to herself, a chicken coop is built to protect the chickens, and there is hay to keep them warm and comfortable. A chicken coop is not guarded by wolves. Out of the corner of her eye she can still see the man in the olive-green dress shirt, the slacks with the blue stripe running down the length of the seam, and the black boots, standing in place watching her. Making sure she does not give in to the urge to rest her weight on her heels. Making sure she does not escape her punishment.

Did they call her father? she wonders. They said they would. She had given them his name and phone number. At least, the last number she had for him, from the last time he had called, on her tenth birthday, when he said he would come back to get her. He promised to bring her to live with him in *El Otro Lado* — the Other Side — and take her to see the place where Selena, her favourite singer ever, had lived. There were so many nice things in Texas that they would see and do together!

"Did you know," Daddy had said over the phone, "that there is an island here waiting especially for us, an island for very cool daddies and daughters to spend time together, called the Father's Island?

"Get out of here!" Magda laughed. "You're joking!"

"It's true, sweetie. It's called *La Isla del Padre*. And when you come, I'll take you to the beach. And then we'll go to Corpus Christi and see everything that has to do with Selena. Deal?"

"Deal!" And the way their laughter blended together had made Magda feel like her daddy was giving her a hug.

She had dreamed of that plan ever since — even toyed with the idea of changing her name to Selena so she could start her new life properly. Selena sounded so much better than Magdalena. And after her last fight with her mother, the fight that had prompted her to leave, Magda felt the urge to reinvent herself as soon as possible. She closes her eyes now and lets her dream identity take over her mind. Selena is a name that screams success: after Selena Quintanilla and Selena Gómez, the world will hear of her,

Selena Farías. She will honour her fallen hero's memory by going back to school and working hard until she can open her own clothing store. And just like Selena Gómez designed a bikini to hide her kidney-transplant scar, she will design tops that hide the size of her breasts. All she needs is for Daddy to come pick her up. He will help her make it all come true.

"Hey, you!" A new guard interrupts her train of thought. "You can get up now."

Magda drops her weight on her heels first, then sits down on the floor. She tries to stretch, but freezes—a different kind of cold—when pain shoots through her leg. After massaging her thighs and knees a little, she tries to stand by pressing her hands against the wall. Every muscle in her legs and back hurts. Her toenails have turned blue. If only she could warm her feet for just five minutes! The room spins a bit once she manages to stand fully erect. More than anything, she wants to rinse out her mouth with fresh water, to brush her teeth, but no one has given them access to toothbrushes or soap. There is dirt under her fingernails. Her armpits exude a rancid odour. Everything and everyone here stinks. Juan Carlitos's hair is stiff, his tears have drawn lines in his dirty cheeks. His knees are scratched and his arms are covered in goose pimples because of the cold. He looks like a plucked chicken. They all do. Plucked chickens in the saddest and cruelest chicken coop in the world. The boy was already thin when they met, but Magda believes he has grown even thinner. What will be left of him if his aunt does not come soon? At least he does not need diapers, Magda tells herself with gratitude when she sees him coming in her direction. Her sense of smell has become fierce. She knows she will forever remember every single odour trapped in this place. She will forever remember every sound. And she will forever remember today's guard.

MAGDA'S STOMACH GROWLS. She is hungry but not sure she will be able to eat if they ever bring food again. All they have been given since their arrival is mouldy sandwiches and instant soup served lukewarm with the noodles only half-cooked, so that eating them feels like chewing on elastic bands. Juan Carlitos has been complaining of a stomach ache. Others have diarrhea, bad coughs, runny noses, rashes. Perhaps even a fever, who knows? No one checks. The guards have instructed the older children to care for the younger ones, but Magda thinks, looking at Juan Carlitos, she is already doing more than her fair share.

"Where's my mommy?" Juan Carlitos looks up, trying to find Magda's eyes.

"She's gone to find your sister and then she'll meet you at your aunt's house, remember?" Magda's eyes avoid his. She is tired of repeating the same answer over and over.

She is starting to believe that it is all a lie, that no one will ever come to save them. Is it daytime? Nighttime? How many days have gone by? There are no answers to her questions. What if they cannot locate her daddy? What then? Whatever happens, she knows she cannot go back home.

"*¡Puta!*" Her mother's voice still echoes in her head. "You're a whore! Look at yourself! Are you trying to steal him from me?" The way her mother stared at her chest hurt like a stab wound.

"Steal *who* from you?"

"Don't play silly with me! Rafael, of course."

"Rafael?" Magda thought her mother was being ridiculous. "He could be my father, what are you talking about?"

"He *could* be your father, but he is *not* your father. Don't pretend you don't see the way he stares at you."

Magda fights back the tears about to be born in her eyes. She has promised herself to appear strong for Juan Carlitos. But every time she recalls this conversation, a wave of sadness threatens to drown her. Her mother knew how much Magda disliked Rafael. She had been against him moving into their house from the beginning. She was still waiting for her daddy, hoping her parents would get back together and live like a couple again. Rafael's arrival had shattered that possibility and Magda hated him for it. Yes, she noticed how he stared at her, but what was she supposed to do? Wear a sweater in that heat?

"You already ruined my life once; I'm not letting you ruin it again." It does not matter how many times Magda replays the scene in her mind, she still hasn't found the right words to reply. She wishes it had all ended there, like so many of her mother's drunken outbursts, but her mother had never lost control that way before.

"When your father named you Magdalena, I knew, I *knew* it was a bad idea. It's a whore's name. And that's exactly what you'll turn out to be. You need to leave."

If it hadn't been for Doña Toñita, she would not have known what to do or where to go. She even gave Magda some money to make her journey easier, and kissed her on the forehead before she left, like a grandmother would have done.

THINKING ABOUT HER mother makes Magda long even more to become Selena. Selena is pure, successful, and loved. Unlike Magdalena, the whore. Everything was supposed to be better in *El Otro Lado*. Doña Toñita told her all she needed to do was reach the border and cross it. Everything would be fine after that. But it was all a lie. All those movies and TV shows that Magda had watched where people showed that they cared about each other were lies. All those movies and TV shows where police officers and soldiers behaved with kindness and generosity were lies.

There is no kindness and generosity to be found here. They don't want anyone who does not look like them and talk like them. This is the real *El Otro Lado*.

"Are you missing your mommy, too?" Juan Carlitos stretches his hand out and tries to dry the tears falling down Magda's cheeks, but she pushes his arm away and he recoils.

"MAGDALENA FARÍAS!" HEARING the guard calling her name put a smile on her face.

"I'm here!" She pushed Juan Carlitos to the side. "Is my daddy here?" Her heart was beating so fast and she felt so excited that her hands started to sweat.

"I need you to follow me, please." The guard held up a blue folder in his hand for her to see. "There's some paperwork we need to complete."

Magda almost exploded with joy and tried to memorize everything about that moment, when she could almost taste freedom. This guard had broad shoulders and was taller than the others. To her, he looked like a movie star. And he smelled so clean and fresh! Perhaps she would ask him what cologne he was wearing, so that she could give it to her daddy as a present and tell him all about this day. The first day of the end of the nightmare. She followed him down a long hallway towards an office at the back. The room was empty except for a table and a chair. Magda was disappointed to see that it did not have a window. She missed seeing the sky! There was a cardboard box with worn file folders on the floor, but she remained focused on the blue folder in the guard's hand. It was the only one that mattered.

Standing in the middle of the room, Magda was expecting him to place the papers on the table for her to see. She did not expect him to lock the door behind them. She did not expect his blue eyes to scrutinize her the way they did, covering her with shame simply by sweeping up and down her body.

"Where's the paperwork?" Magda's knees were shaking, her hands wet.

"It's up to you to make it flow faster, Chiquita." The way he pronounced the word *Chiquita* made Magda shiver. She saw his zipper going down and felt trapped in the scariest part of a fairy tale: she was about to be eaten by the wolf. Her attempt to reach the door was fruitless—he was faster and stronger than her—and before Magda could defend herself or find her voice to scream, he had already pushed her down on her knees, placed his hands on her head, and pulled her face towards his crotch.

PERHAPS HER MOTHER is right, Magda ponders. Why else would that guard have chosen her from among all the other girls in the pen? If only her breasts were smaller, easier to hide, perhaps nothing would have happened. It could have been worse, however. If she had eaten more, for example. Vomiting in the officer's lap would have been even worse then. And her punishment could have been worse, too. Magda's legs are still numb after kneeling for so long against the wall, but she knows it could have been worse. Her head is throbbing, she cannot stand the noise anymore, cannot stand the cold anymore, cannot think anymore, does not want to remember anymore. She bites her fist to muffle a cry of anger and despair. She does it so as not to wake up Juan Carlitos, who is miraculously asleep, not because she is afraid that anyone will identify her cry amidst the symphony of wails that hang in the air like icicles about to break.

Uncle Ko's One Thousand Lives

For Ko Un

WHEN NO ONE expected his return anymore, when almost everyone believed he must be dead, he appeared out of nowhere at our door. He had always been slim, but now it seemed as though his skin were the only thing holding his bones in place. As if, in that body of his, there was neither blood nor muscles nor tendons, just skeleton and hide inexplicably joined together. His eyes, larger than ever, welled up with tears when he saw me, but I did not recognize him. He scared me and I screamed, and Mother was about to push him away thinking he was a drifter, a madman. How could we have ever imagined it was Uncle Ko! When I finally hugged him, I could feel his vertebrae, his shoulder blades sticking out like rocks on a desert plain. His body resembled the moonscape: there were craters, protuberances, changes in tone and texture that belonged to a different world. He was wearing a very light cotton shirt, stained with dirt and dry blood, and his skin was cold. Moist and cold, like a frog's. The sun was about to set, it was breezy, and yet his hair did not respond to the wind's rhythm. It remained stiff. What did they do to him? I couldn't ask. Words tied themselves in a knot in my throat, tangled together with my anguish. I was afraid he'd lose his balance, I thought he was going to crumble; I just couldn't understand how those feet, whose bones seemed to compete against one another to see which one would be the most visible, could keep him standing up.

Uncle Ko was a poet. Mother had told me that ever since he was a child, he would spend hours looking for new words to name beauty and fear, and that he seemed to find them just lingering in the air at the very instant he needed them. When he started school, his teacher recognized immediately that she would never have another pupil like Ko, and she convinced my grandparents to allow him to lose himself in the pages of every available book. Sickly and scrawny as he was, Grandma thought it was prudent to follow his teacher's advice and, while Mother helped around home, Uncle Ko read. He always carried a notebook, and within its covers he used up every possible inch of paper to rehearse images, similes, and metaphors. I know it for a fact because I have that notebook, the first one. The rest were burned the day they came to arrest him, but that first one was already hidden beneath a loose wooden board under my bed. I never tired of looking at it, of guessing the emotions that his calligraphy laid bare, of watching in awe how he sailed through language like someone who, after wading in furious waters, had finally arrived at a calm river and then, slowly, reached the sea. I know this, too, because when Uncle Ko realized that my hands were too clumsy for anything except holding a pen and using it to create worlds that turned like his, he made me his apprentice. Right up until the day he was taken away. I was nine years old, and I cried for many days after because the same night that I lost him, his notebooks and my notebooks also perished—consumed in the fire, together with all the books he had promised to let me read when I was older. A dark scar in the middle of our courtyard was all that was left behind. That, and the empty shelves and broken bookcases that Father did not dare repair, and which we discarded with the garbage in the following weeks.

Nobody had explained to me that Uncle Ko's poems were considered a dangerous weapon. Who would have guessed? The foreigners who came to visit him always spoke highly of his work; they took with them copies of his writings to publish in languages that we could not understand and, sometimes, they asked him to go on trips with them. Whenever Uncle Ko accepted their invitations, my sole consolation was to know that he would return to me supplied with new books and stories.

After the soldiers took Uncle Ko away, Father went out searching for him in all the city's jails and hospitals, but his efforts were futile. Mother ultimately felt glad that Grandpa and Grandma were no longer alive, and therefore would not share her anguish and the piercing pain of not knowing what had happened to her brother. After months of inquiries, of going from one office to the next, always in vain, my parents gave up their search. I realized then that they were scared of being connected to Uncle Ko. Later, however, their fear transformed into forgetfulness and habit, and hundreds of days went by without questions or tears. Until the afternoon when Uncle Ko returned.

Once inside the house, Uncle Ko asked for a cup of tea. Instead of sitting down, he remained standing, looking around the room slowly and taking us in, one by one, Mother, Father, and me—especially me—without haste, as if drinking us up with his gaze. He had lost several teeth, and the ones that remained were rotten, but the frank laughter that exploded in his face filled us with joy and curiosity.

"What are you laughing about?" Mother asked, trying to laugh as well, in spite of the tears with which she had been suddenly overcome. Her eyes changed for an instant and, if only fleetingly, I caught the look of the little girl who had grown up with Ko and who was glad to have him back, no matter the condition.

"I'm laughing at how well I remembered your nose and your voice and all the colours in this room."

None of us understood what he meant, but we smiled regardless. Mother helped him sit down in an armchair. His frog skin stretched instead of ripping, as I was expecting it would, and Uncle Ko then proceeded to drink his tea in silence. We couldn't stop staring at him. We were anxious to pummel him with an avalanche of questions, but we did not dare. Finally, Uncle Ko pointed at the cup he was holding between his fingers and said:

"I was held in a place so dark that I couldn't even see the edge of a cup such as this."

We didn't know what to say, how to respond, until I followed my instincts and went to fetch him some paper and a pen. Uncle Ko took the pen and held it carefully in his fingers, as if doubting its existence, and then, as if he had forgotten what it was used for. He spent a few minutes looking at it and caressing it before putting it to paper. When he tried to write, his wrist betrayed him, and he couldn't form even a single letter. The pain that suddenly convulsed his face told us what he had suffered.

Many weeks went by before Uncle Ko recovered his strength. I thought writing would help him heal faster and encouraged him to try again, but the pen kept slipping out of his fingers and he complained that his wrist ached. Watching his eyes turn sombre forced me to find another way to coax out the words that, caught in a maelstrom, had accumulated inside him and were waiting for an opportunity to emerge. That's how it occurred to me to transcribe his words. Uncle Ko initially refused. He feared he would be imprisoned again and drag me down with him. It took me several days to convince him that this could be our secret. No one at home, not even my parents, would find out.

We worked together, in secrecy, when I came home from school and he from his wanderings around the neighbourhood. If anyone asked about his poetry, he showed them his clumsy, stiff fingers. Nobody believed him dangerous anymore. We were careful. And, to avoid a repetition of his previous fate and the destruction of our work, I carefully hid page after page under the same loose wooden plank that had protected his notebook. We knew that nothing could be done with the poems until the regime fell, but that never discouraged us.

That is how I learned that he had consoled himself during his confinement by evoking the features of every person he had ever met. And he had made himself a promise that if he survived his ordeal and was ever free again, he would write a poem about every person who had crossed his path. One such poem was about the woman who repaired old shoes in our village. I knew her silver braids very well and was acquainted with the vinegary smell of the curtains that hung from her shop window and lingered on her clothes. But Uncle Ko revealed to me the coarse texture of her hands and the curve of her back in a way I had never seen before. Another poem revolved around his grandmother's last words, asking for the lining of her husband's coat to be fixed. It was through these poems that I understood the depth of simplicity. Others, however, were about those people whose screams he had heard in the jail but whose faces he never saw. Sometimes he made me cry for the entire afternoon, but he kept insisting, *Don't cry, my girl. Let us write...*

There are more than a thousand lives that Uncle Ko shared with me and left behind on paper, sung by his voice and transcribed by my hand during my late adolescence. More than a thousand are the pages that survived in hiding. And now that our country is at last free, it is only fair to liberate his poems from their lengthy imprisonment. Uncle Ko would have liked this book so much! That is why I am here today, standing in his place—I, who learned everything from him—and here are these *Thousand Lives* to demand justice as only poetry can; to reveal those who went on living simple lives, and those who were condemned to darkness, and to bring to life the memories that saved us—him from madness, and his people from oblivion.

Fiat voluntas Dei

SHE EXITS THE car and slams the driver's door shut. Her knees are shaking as she approaches the café where they have agreed to meet. Trying to be discreet, she steps inside, but is aware that, more than her clothes — a red miniskirt and low-cut blouse, an outfit she chose on purpose — it's her limp that will catch the other patrons' attention. It's better now than it used to be, when people used to stare at her without trying to hide their curiosity or their pity, but she still feels uneasy before entering an unfamiliar place. Especially this one, this place, today.

Her heels click unevenly against the tile floor. Relieved to discover that the café is essentially empty, she heads towards the counter and orders a large, extra-dark coffee, no cream. A black drink to match her mood. Should she have worn black to this meeting? It would show that she's still in mourning, even after all these years. No. She shakes her head to shoo away the thought like a fly. Black would be read as pious. Red, however, symbolizes self-confidence and bravery, which is what she needs right now.

She takes a seat by the window and puts down her cup. She looks out at the carefree people strolling along the sidewalk, the cars negotiating an intricate choreography in the parking lot, and the sun, indifferent and obscene, crowning a pristine blue sky. He will surely take that as a sign in his favour, but to her it feels like a personal affront. Today should be overcast, rainy. The burnished golden flowers in the planters, the lofty, thickly leaved trees are almost an insult.

She places her purse on her lap, her left arm cradling it tightly. She looks at the clock on the wall. Nine fifty. If he doesn't arrive on time, she'll leave. She takes a sip of her coffee to check the temperature. It's still scalding hot and burns her lips and tongue. But she doesn't mind. That her pain threshold is higher than average is something she has been aware of for a very long time.

A woman with salt-and-pepper hair emerges from the washroom and takes a seat at the table next to her. Why do people enjoy crowding perfect strangers? she wonders. The only other customer is a young man hunched over on a couch at the back of the café, wearing headphones and typing on his laptop. He looks like he could be roughly her age, in his early twenties, but in contrast to her, his movements are self-assured, his confidence real. A wave of contempt rises and breaks inside her chest. He probably never had to carry his belongings inside a black garbage bag from one home to the next. He probably thinks everyone had a nice, safe upbringing, just like his, coddled in his parents' embrace, wanting for nothing. That must be why he seems so self-absorbed. The woman next to her unfolds her newspaper noisily, spreading it out as though she were about to perform an autopsy. Why do people always go to cafés to read the newspaper or work on their computers? They don't get to choose the music (right now, the corniest love song ever written is blasting through tinny speakers above the counter) and they end up sitting next to the smelly washroom, like that guy in the back. Why do people choose that? She would never be able to work here, not even by the window, where the smell of cookie dough, coffee, and freshly baked pastries is appealing. On any other day she would've purchased a croissant, but right now she can't even imagine taking a bite.

Ten minutes later, at ten o'clock sharp, the glass door opens. And there he is. Predictably dressed in black, impeccable shoes, a silver beard — no longer auburn — that is groomed exactly the way she remembers it. Their eyes meet, but only he smiles. As he walks towards her, his body language roars power and control. She understands that she is expected to rise to her feet and give him a hug, but she stays put, her left hand on her purse and her right around the cardboard sleeve of her coffee. She tries to feign indifference, but drops of sweat bead on the back of her neck. In a conscious effort to prevent her knees from betraying her, she places her feet firmly on the floor as she examines his face, a face she recalled and feared for so long that it has become less like a real man's face and more like a vision from a nightmare.

"Good morning." She holds his stare.

"It's such a blessing to see you again. Thank God that you came." His voice is assertive and deep. He sits in the chair across from her and theatrically draws out a handkerchief to wipe a drop of moisture from his eye. "Thank you for agreeing to see me, Rosario."

The sound of her old name coming from his mouth and that aqueous gaze give her whiplash. She responds by clenching her teeth and sitting taller. How convenient it must be to cry that easily, she thinks, as her mind slides down the tunnel of memory towards those everlasting nights spent in fear and pain.

"It hurts!" She remembers her voice going hoarse from her desperate pleas for help.

"Brothers and sisters, let us pray that God grants this child of ours the strength to overcome this test."

Hands would be held together and prayers would be

mumbled, but the pain would not subside. It only ever increased. Who showed any pity for her back then?

She watches in silence now as he dabs his eyes with the handkerchief.

"Don't call me Rosario. My name is Violeta." Her voice comes out strong, makes her feel proud of herself.

The man stares at her as if he doesn't understand, but she knows better than to take the bait.

"Aren't you getting a coffee?" She feels a sudden urge to delay their conversation, even by just a few moments.

The man nods. As he rises, he pushes his chair back noisily. The newspaper woman sitting next to them turns her head with curiosity. Violeta shoots her a look that says, What are you looking at? and the woman goes back to her paper. She is reading the obituaries. Very apropos, Violeta thinks. It takes the man only a couple of minutes to return, a ceramic mug of tea in his hands, which he holds carefully so as not to spill it. It must be very hot. He sits down again, this time trying not to make too much noise with his chair. They sit together in silence, staring at each other. His frown lets her know that her outfit has had the desired effect. 1-0, and the match has only just begun.

"I brought you a present." He produces a white box from his pocket and places it on top of the table, expecting her to reach for it. Violeta is aware that the newspaper woman is watching them out of the corner of her eye. The computer guy from the back has just gone to the counter to buy another coffee. Violeta doesn't know whether to satisfy the man's eagerness—and the woman's curiosity—or make them wait. She decides to wait until the guy returns to his seat and dons his headphones again. Only then will she make a move. Every second's delay is a small victory. ·

"Don't you want to see what it is?"

"Not interested."

"I've had this for years, waiting for an opportunity to give it to you. Please, open it, Rosario."

"No."

At this point he becomes visibly angry—his temples throb—but Violeta knows he will not make a scene in public. She's not worried. The box remains on the table and becomes a kind of barrier between them. Scoreboard: 2-0 in her favour, 3-0, if she takes into consideration that her knees are no longer shaking and she's stopped sweating.

"It's a rosary. Blessed by the pope himself. I brought it for you from Rome. I've been keeping it all these years, waiting for the chance to give it to you." On the surface his tone is conciliatory, but his supressed anger is a shark lurking in the depths of his eyes.

Violeta shrugs and takes a little sip of her coffee. It's still hot, so she blows on it to cool it down, as if she were trying to snuff out a votive candle.

"Don't you pray anymore?"

She shakes her head and is about to tell him that she doesn't believe in anything anymore, but stops herself because that's not entirely true. She believes in love beyond death because that's the kind of love she feels for Ezequiel. And she believes in human justice, imperfect but attainable. But no, she doesn't pray. And she doesn't believe in God or the established church or any of that insidious absurdity.

"I didn't expect you to abandon your faith."

Her faith? More like her condemnation.

He leans forward to make sure she understands the importance of what he's saying. "I never imagined that being away from us would lead you to step away from the Truth."

He pauses for effect. She's determined not to take the bait. So instead she merely sighs. He'll need to up his game.

He changes tack. "I've missed you." Violeta clenches her teeth. "And I'm sure you've missed us, too."

Does she miss the women in ankle-length skirts whose minds belonged in the Middle Ages? The women who followed his every instruction blindly, going against their basic common sense? Does she miss the fasting, the lack of human comforts "to please the Lord"? Does she miss the praying before sunrise, before every meal, before every breath? She takes a sip of her coffee but suddenly feels nauseous and pushes the cup away from her.

"Is this why you've been badgering me to see you?" She is making a superhuman effort not to raise her voice. What he missed was not her, but his power over her. The man leans towards her, as though to whisper something in her ear, but she flinches instinctively backwards.

"There's still time to save your soul, my child. You know that is my sacred duty."

Violeta lets out a guffaw that catches even the barista's attention. She doesn't care anymore, but the man looks mortified. Mortified and furious.

"*You* want to save *me*?"

The man stares at her with determination while he brings his right hand to his forehead, chest, left and right shoulder — the same exaggerated, theatrical sign of the cross that she remembers so well.

"You must forgive and forget the past. It's the Word." His conciliatory tone doesn't conceal the volcano that is about to erupt from inside him. Violeta is surprised to discover how well she still knows him. She's glad to be in a public place. When she was little, when Ezequiel was still alive, this was the kind of gaze — the kind of tone — that preceded a beating. Like the one that had left her with a broken leg. Her treatment? Horsetail, arnica, dandelion leaf, turmeric, a homemade splint, and prayer.

"Take me to a doctor, please, I'm in pain!" she had asked. No, not asked. Begged.

"A doctor will only prescribe you toxic chemicals. You're better off with the natural medicine given to us by the Lord."

Violeta feels the urge to stretch her leg, to kick that memory away, but continues to sit still, clutching her purse tighter instead. Her limp is nothing compared to what Ezequiel had to endure. Yes, it's the perfect moment to bring up the only thing she wants to talk about, the only memory she needs to revisit. She opens her purse and brings out an object wrapped in blue crepe paper. A hand-print pressed into clay. The print of a tiny hand.

"Remember this?"

The man grimaces. Scoreboard: 4-0. Violeta holds his gaze, and for the first time he looks down at the floor.

"It's Ezequiel's." She revels in the blow she has just struck, even though she is now short of breath as well. He remains silent but his trembling chin betrays his emotion. Violeta places Ezequiel's clay handprint on the table, centimetres away from the box with the rosary.

"Why didn't you save him?"

The man grabs his handkerchief from his breast pocket and fidgets for a moment. Finally, after pretending to dry his face, he gives her a look that reminds her of a wounded animal.

"I did everything I could to save him," he wheedles. "You simply don't remember. You were only seven."

"I may have been seven but I remember what you did." Although her tone is openly accusatory, she tries to keep her voice down.

"Then you must know that we gave him every treatment we knew of. We took the best possible care of him. We prayed non-stop. We offered him to the Divine Grace." His voice cracks, but he coughs slightly and regains his composure. "It was God's will, and the ways of God are unfathomable."

Violeta clenches her fists until her fingers hurt. The sound of a door closing startles her. The guy at the back has gone into the washroom. Her heart is beating like she has just run a marathon.

"And why would God give meningitis to a four-year-old?" She is genuinely eager to know, but her voice seasons her question with a pinch of involuntary sarcasm.

"To teach us a lesson in humility and faith — a truth that you have obviously forgotten." This is the same tone of voice that made her cry when she was little. Violeta turns to stone. Suddenly she's a small girl again; she feels that if she says anything she will crumble. She resists the impulse to scream that what he's saying is bullshit, that she may have been seven years old but she knew full well that Ezequiel didn't die to teach them a lesson but because he was left alone with a high fever for several days. Because when he first fell ill and didn't recover, when the fever wouldn't subside, instead of taking him to the hospital, the man forced him to drink herbal teas and eat radishes and garlic drenched in honey, which were supposed to cure him, and when he couldn't even drink anymore he was fed those concoctions with a spoon and then a dropper, until his brain became so swollen that his tiny body was rigid, and hugging him was like hugging a hot wooden board.

Violeta remembers how Ezequiel was burning hot to the touch. She remembers the last moments she spent with him, holding him, listening to his erratic breathing. How it suddenly stopped, and her heart skipped a beat as she patted him on the back until he finally gasped for air. When she laid him on the bed to go fetch help, he stopped breathing again. Her yelling alerted their father, the man now sitting in front of her, the man whose name she had vowed never to pronounce again. She will never forget how he pinched Ezequiel's little nose, blew into his mouth to get him coughing—a lightning bolt of hope that was immediately extinguished.

She had planned to confront him, to yell in his face that he was a criminal, a murderer, but her words had been lost hiding from the presence that made her so afraid during her childhood. The man offers her his handkerchief and that's when Violeta realizes she's crying. She rejects his offer, wipes her nose and eyes with the back of her hand, and hates herself. Scoreboard: 4–1, but that 1 counts for 4. They're even.

"Rosario, come back where you belong. Don't torture yourself with those memories anymore. It was God's will, and that is that. It's not our place to question His ways."

The tenderness in the man's gaze sets Violeta's voice free, and it rushes out with the impetuosity of thunder.

"Was it also God's will for my broken leg to be cured with natural ointments, condemning me to limp forever? And my name is Violeta, not Rosario, motherfucker!" She startles even herself. That's not a word in her regular vocabulary. But it feels good. Oh my, it feels good to spit it out at him. And even if she's lost the energy to keep count, she knows that she's winning. The newspaper woman, whose pretence of reading the obituaries has now disappeared completely, opens her mouth in shock. The barista, equally startled, looks over at them in surprise. The man challenges them all with his eyes and makes a gesture with his hand, warning them not to intervene. And they freeze. It is the first time as an adult that Violeta can see the effect this man has on others, not just on her. The woman blushes, mutters an excuse, and turns back to her newspaper. The barista turns his back on them. Only then does the man return his attention to Violeta.

"I did what I thought was best: I trusted in God. You know doctors are not to be trusted. Not after what they did to your mother."

Violeta bites her lower lip in disbelief. How dare he? He was the one who established the rule, the rule about not speaking about her mother, a rule that Violeta still follows to this day. This is low even for him. It deserves a red card. She grabs her purse and makes as if to stand, but he looks ready to go after her and this is not how things are supposed to go.

"As I said, it is not our place to question the ways of the Lord."

Trying to stick to her plan and summon what little strength she has left, Violeta takes a deep breath.

"So it was God and not you who murdered Ezequiel. Is that what you're saying?"

The man thrusts himself forward, his hands gripping the table with such strength that his fingertips turn white and the veins in his neck swell. Violeta wishes she hadn't agreed to this meeting and takes a furtive look towards the exit.

"I need another coffee." She gets up and walks to the counter without completely turning her back to the man. She needs to regain her composure, but she also needs to watch him. Her heels inadvertently keep time with the rhythm of the mellow song playing in the background. She takes a deep breath and smiles at the barista.

"Large coffee. To go, please." He smiles back at her as she pays. The drink is so hot that a double sleeve is required. Her eyes lock with the man's as she retakes her seat at the table and places the cup next to Ezequiel's handprint.

"What I'm saying is that I'd like you to come home with me. I should never have allowed you to go, for us to be separated. We're your family."

Violeta shakes her head, retrieves the handprint and

wraps it carefully in the blue crepe paper. Before returning it to her purse, she lifts it up for the man to see.

"I wouldn't be alive if they hadn't separated us. Don't you understand that they took me away so you wouldn't do to me what you did to Ezequiel?" Her words conjure up the memory of her little brother's stiff body. "He would've lived if you had taken him to see a doctor. Bacterial meningitis cannot be cured with radishes and prayers, but it can be cured with antibiotics. How can you live with yourself? Do you remember how he cried? The pain he was in? The pain that *you* inflicted upon him? He was only four!"

She suddenly rises to her feet. The man reaches out to try to stop her, but Violeta dodges his arm. He rakes her up and down with a scathing look of disapproval.

"Forgiveness is a wondrous gift. I have forgiven you, my child. And God has forgiven me. We're still in time to free you from all your sins."

Violeta lets out a bitter laugh.

"*You* have forgiven *me*?"

The man nods.

"And God has forgiven *you*?"

The man nods again. She considers this for a moment.

"That means you have repented. So you *do* admit you were wrong?"

The veins in the man's neck make her think of fat little snakes.

"Never mind. Everything that happens is God's will, right?"

Violeta doesn't allow the panic brewing in her stomach to paralyze her. This time she forces herself to be brave. She picks up the cup of hot coffee and swiftly removes the lid.

"God wants this for you today." She throws its content in the man's face before he can lift his hands for protection. He yells in pain and swears at her. The newspaper woman jumps to her feet, screaming. The barista hesitates behind the counter, unsure what to do.

"A present from God, in Ezequiel's name!" Limping as fast as she can, Violeta leaves the café without looking back. She's afraid the newspaper woman, the computer guy, or the barista will try to stop her, but no one comes after her.

Once she's safely out of the parking lot and back on the highway, she begins to feel her back relax against the seat; her neck and shoulders and even her fingers hurt. Her jaw and her temples feel painful too, although not as much as his face. His face must be hurting. And that thought makes her smile.

Dear Abuela

IT'S MID-SEPTEMBER. A few copper leaves lie scattered
on the pavement announcing the end of summer. Drops
of sweat are sliding down my back as I write you this
letter in an effort to find calm. I don't know what else
to do. My jaw hurts from clenching my teeth to stop my
voice. Will you mind if my tears rain on these pages,
if my writing becomes unintelligible? Today, my pen is
dripping sorrow.

It's been fourteen hours since I received the news.
Fourteen hours and twenty-three minutes. I don't know
why I'm counting, it's absurd, but I cannot stop staring at
the time—at my phone, which won't ring again. I could
have rushed to the airport to catch the one daily direct
flight from Toronto to Mexico City. I would have arrived
hours ago. I'd be in the convent right now, assisting the

nuns, attending your wake. But what good would my presence have been, really? Would it have made any difference if I was there to say goodbye now that you're gone, when I wasn't there to hold your hand as you lay dying?

The silence that engulfs me turns the air into crystal splinters. It hurts to breathe.

Toronto was your idea, Abuela. You promised you'd catch up with me as soon as I found my footing. In spite of the weather, you said. You were never scared of anything except cold weather. I remember you telling me that it was mid-January when you were forced to leave the house you grew up in. The wind was so fierce that day that it engraved its memory in your bones. Okay, to be fair, there was something else you were afraid of besides the cold: soldiers. Cold weather and the army are the two most dangerous things in the world, you said, always most brutal towards those most vulnerable.

It was precisely because of the weather that I suggested Vancouver. Rain is better than snow; right, Abuela? But you insisted that Toronto was the safer bet. It's the best place for your professional development, Hija, you said. I thought the same and, once here, I didn't have the heart to disappoint you. In truth, I haven't been able to get certified as a librarian. To survive, I've been working as a cashier in a supermarket since my arrival. Earning a living in this place is much more difficult than we imagined. And there is nothing in this landscape, similar to that of your childhood in Poland, that can comfort me.

We didn't want luxuries, only safety and peace.

The good news? Safety and peace do exist here, Abuela.

The bad news? They come at a hefty price: unbearable solitude.

People here are always surprised when I say I'm Mexican—apparently, I don't look the part. Do they expect me to wear a sombrero? Or do they believe all Mexicans look the same? That's why I never mention that I was born in Buenos Aires. That would be too confusing, and I don't remember anything about our life in Argentina anyway. Time and again you described to me the apartment in San Telmo and told me how much I loved feeding the ducks in Palermo, but I've forgotten it all.

We arrived in Mexico City carrying only one suitcase, my teddy bear, and our treasures—family souvenirs that proved we hadn't always been alone. Black-and-white photographs that eased my childhood anxieties: I do have Papi's nose, don't I, Abuela? Can you style my hair like Mami's? You smiled and allowed me to keep some of those old photos under my pillow when I slept. That's exactly how you, too, used to soothe yourself to sleep after arriving with your father in Argentina at the end of the war. You both rebuilt your lives in the sweltering Buenos Aires summer, learning a new language and a new way of life. The Río de la Plata looked less like a river and more like a placid, muddy sea, unlike the Vistula, but its waters managed to lull your nostalgia for Warsaw... until you learned that in those waters they had dumped the bodies of thousands of *desaparecidos*. Perhaps even Papi's? We never found out for sure. If the authorities don't have answers for the mothers, surely they won't have them for the mothers-in-law.

Perhaps everything happened as a punishment. Perhaps I deserved it for being selfish. I lacked the courage to help you carry our past and instead let you bear its weight on your own. I don't have any memory of Papi, neither of his voice nor his smell. I only know he was taller and bigger than me because of that sweater of his you saved for me. When you told me that he used to read me stories at night and that it was he who instilled in me my love of books, Abuela, I pretended to remember, but my mind was blank. I could conjure no images except for those trapped in the photographs my eyes were never too tired to look at. A blurry black-and-white face, large glasses, unruly hair. With Mami it's different. I never dared say this out loud to you, but don't you think it's almost a blessing that she passed away when I was a baby? At least we know what happened to her and where she is buried.

Abuela, you used to say that history is round, that's why it repeats itself. In the same way that your father took you from Warsaw at the height of winter, you and I left Buenos

Aires on a dull and frigid July evening. Mexico's sunshine welcomed us with open arms. Remember your first job? How proud you were to have been hired as a bilingual secretary; how excited I was to attend kindergarten. We met our neighbours, started making friends — but not with other Argentinians. You had learned that a group of Argentinian refugees organized get-togethers every so often. We went to one once but left almost immediately. It was because you couldn't stand the sadness. You didn't want to hold on to the past. You chose to surround us with people who didn't talk about politics.

And so we dived deep into Mexican culture. For several weekends we visited the Museo Nacional de Antropología and, one hall at a time, we learned to admire the greatness of the Aztecs, the Mayans, and the Toltecs. We visited the pyramids, marvelled at the murals of Diego Rivera and the marine landscapes by Clausell, and I lost myself in the worlds created by Remedios Varo. Just like us, you said, she had arrived in Mexico searching for peace, and had found it. How lucky for the three of us, to have found such paradise.

How generous you were, Abuela. What mattered most to you was that I receive the best possible education. I remember how you monitored my schoolwork every night and helped me study. Don't think for a moment that I wasn't aware you wanted me to become a doctor, but when I chose to become a librarian you still supported me. How could

I have chosen a different path? After all, we never tired
of flipping through the pages of the encyclopedia that we
had at home. Since we couldn't afford the luxury of travelling abroad, we travelled the world through its pages,
photographs, and coordinates. And yes, we did take some
beautiful road trips. Abuela, you gifted me this wonderful
country. I cannot believe that you're dead and I'm so far
away.

THE CAR RIDE with my head pressed between a dirty floor-
mat and the barrel of a gun changed everything. Abuela,
you were right. History is round; it repeats itself. In the
same way Papi had been taken, I was then taken myself.
Who would have imagined? Even if their reasons were not
political, those who aimed their guns at me were as criminal as the Argentinian soldiers who supported the military
junta. Take the car, I implored, take my purse, take everything, but please don't hurt me; please, please let me go.
They laughed. Look at this *mamacita*, what a *chula guerita*.
Your boyfriend is a lucky motherfucker. But I didn't have a
boyfriend; I had never had a boyfriend. I had devoted myself
to books. I told them so, and they laughed even harder.

I never told you this, Abuela, but sometimes I can still
detect the stench of that room on my skin. It doesn't matter
how hard I scrub myself in the shower; I still feel those

fingers pressing into my body. I still wake up with the feeling of a foreign weight over me, a stranger's breath panting against my ear. I wish I could peel off my skin, but I'm a coward. I've tried, but it hurts so much, and I hate myself for stopping. I hate myself too because even here, where it's safe, I don't go out at night. I don't have friends.

One time I tried therapy for other survivors of torture and abuse, but I couldn't cope. It made everything worse, much worse. I don't know why I never told you, Abuela. Please forgive me for lying to you all this time. There was a Congolese woman in the group whose hands had been chopped off when a band of rebels invaded her village. I can't shake from my memory the way she wiped her tears with her stumps. This is Toronto, Abuela, there are people here from all over the world, and some of them have gone through unimaginable hardship. Another woman told us how she had seen her entire family die under the burst of machine guns; she escaped only because they wanted to keep her as a sex slave. The UN had liberated her recently and an NGO helped to relocate her here. Her voice was cavernous, as if it were coming from another world. There was a mother whose daughter had been the victim of an honour killing; her husband and son were in jail. But the worst was the woman from India, the one whose husband had tried to burn her alive. I fixated on her hands, shapeless under thick bandages. The pain she must have endured.

When it was my turn to speak, I wasn't able to say anything. My life, my pain, seemed insignificant compared to theirs. I felt I had no right to be there with them, so I left the meeting early and in shame. I wouldn't have been able to utter the defilement of my body, to describe the theft of my faith. It would have been impossible to explain how much our country had changed—the country that had seemed like paradise but is now a lawless purgatory. I've been worried sick ever since that day thinking about what might happen. If my case is measured against theirs, I stand no chance. What judge will care that I'm startled when people stand too close to me? Who will care that my body was violated by a group of men who held me captive and robbed us of the little we had? If they reject my claim, Abuela, then what? You will have died alone in vain.

I should stop to wipe my tears. My eyes are swollen, my hand sore. I wish I could leave this room, but it's getting dark and I don't like the dark, not even here in Toronto, the city chosen by you because the countryside around it reminded you of Warsaw. The beautiful autumns you described assured me that it would be worth it to put up with the cold of winter. Coming here would be a way to close the family circle and stop history from repeating itself. I couldn't continue to be a citizen of Fear, you said. Here I'd be far away from all the bad memories. The problem is that, along with the bad memories, the good ones have also stayed behind, and from a distance they both hurt the same.

YOU WERE SUPPOSED to catch up with me, Abuela. You promised. Why couldn't you hold on for just a little bit longer? I wish you hadn't used all of our savings to cover my ransom. When I found out how much money you had paid, I held back a scream. How was it possible for so much pain to cost us everything we had and, at the same time, be worth so little?

You know I arrived in Toronto carrying only one suitcase. You know which treasures I brought along, these things that mean everything to me: family photographs, Papi's large sweater, an image of the Virgin of Częstochowa — Poland's patron saint — and your silver necklace with an image of the Virgin of Guadalupe, the only valuable possession you hadn't sold, so that you could give it to me when I was set free.

I still remember your face when you opened the door. Your eyes opened wide, you could hardly believe it was me. I never told you how I made it back. You didn't need to know how they had forced me into the car trunk, bound and gagged, and that I had soiled myself thinking that was the end: mine would be another body found rotting inside an abandoned car. Would they torture me before they killed me? Would they shoot me or stab me? Would they rape me again before killing me? The car drove fast on bumpy roads, probably unpaved. I had no control over my body and I hit my head several times. Music played loudly during the entire ride. The trunk, lined with old newspapers, smelled of gasoline. It was dark except for a dim ray of light that came in through the speakers, and so hot that after a while I thought I might die of suffo-cation. They stopped at the side of a road—I found out later it was after midnight—pulled me out of the trunk, took off the gag and the ropes that bound my hands and feet, and left me there. "You're lucky, *mamacita;* we took pity on your old lady, but if you tell the police we won't have mercy."

I've followed the news from here. Murders, kidnappings, shootings have increased and worsened since I left. The president brought the army in to assist with surveillance and security in the fight against organized crime and the drug cartels. You mentioned this with horror during one of our last conversations. I can still hear your words: "I'm so glad you left, *Hija.* One must always run away the moment the soldiers come out onto the streets. If only my parents had left Warsaw on time, and if your Papi hadn't wanted to change the world and had listened to me when I asked him to flee Buenos Aires, everything would have been different. I'm so happy you listened to me. So happy."

I never got around to asking you this, Abuela, but did you ever wonder what kind of paintings Remedios Varo would have created if she could have seen Mexico now?

THE MOMENT THE phone rang, I knew something was wrong. We only spoke on Sundays. At least you died quickly, without pain—a heart attack probably, not surprising at your age, they said. It's been seventeen hours and forty-six minutes since the call. Who will be at your wake besides the nuns? After my kidnapping we stopped seeing our friends. We stopped being ourselves. I left without telling anyone. And now you no longer are, and no one will remember you except for me, except for me and one day, perhaps, whoever is patient enough to follow the sorrow that dripped from my pen onto this letter.

The First Piano

For my mother, forever the bearer of this gift.

WHEN THE TRUCK appeared on the dusty road, Pedrito ran back into town shouting, "It's here! It's here!" The people began to emerge from their homes and suddenly the square in front of the church was filled with men, women, and children waiting anxiously. Father Domingo joined them, sharing their enthusiasm, calling everyone by name, and enjoying the children, who were running and jumping like crickets, their happy noise brightening the colourless morning. The truck approached on the dirt path, still unpaved even after three politicians in three different elections had promised that they would build a proper street, and came to a slow stop. The driver, short and plump, stepped down from the truck and greeted Father Domingo, bowing his head in respect. His forehead was varnished with sweat, his shirt stained and wrinkled.

"I'm sorry for the delay, Father, but I thought I wasn't going to make it up that road," he said, wiping his forehead with the back of his hand. "I had to drive around a few tree trunks here and there, you know what I mean?"

"I know exactly what you mean, Cástulo." Father Domingo frowned. "I'm sorry to hear that."

Until now, no one coming to town during the day had run into trouble, but Father Domingo was aware that the peace granted to them was fragile. He let out a sigh of relief. "I knew God would not let you come to any serious trouble along the way."

"Well, I just hope Federico is as lucky as I was. He's bringing the lady in your car, isn't he?" Father Domingo nodded, and Cástulo continued, "On top of the roadblocks, the potholes are big enough now to swallow a car in just a bite, you know, Father."

"They'll be here on time, I'm sure, my son." Father Domingo smiled. He knew Cástulo loved to be dramatic.

"I wouldn't blame the lady if she cancelled at the last min—"

"Isn't he going to open the truck, Father? Hurry up!" Pedrito interrupted, and the other children formed a choir echoing his voice.

"Come, my son. Open the truck and help us unload the piano." Father Domingo put his arm around Cástulo's shoulders as they walked to the back of the truck, and the rest of the people followed.

For six weeks, Father Domingo had been talking to them about what was going to take place that afternoon. During a trip to the city to seek support for his parish, he had met Cristina, a young pianist—"a prodigy," he was told—and he had asked her to give a recital in his little church. She had recently returned from abroad after completing her degree in music. He explained how hard people worked in his town. Many of the men had left to try their luck in the city or across the border. Women had been left behind to toil in land as thick as leather, raising children whose only options were migration or the army. He didn't mention the word "cartel"; he had assumed she would understand. Everybody knew that "army" and "cartel" were words that thrived in their symbiotic relationship, especially in that region of the country. One could not exist without the other, and it was people like them, like his flock, who suffered the consequences. He described to her how unforgiving his people's days were, one after the other full of hardships; dry days and burning nights; cockfights and drinking in the only cantina; minds and spirits wasting away after dusk watching telenovelas or Narcos stories, longing for a world they could not explore.

"Our town is a bit far away, and we would not be able to pay you to come," Father Domingo had said, looking a little ashamed. "But we would be able to provide you with safe transport and overnight accommodation. Would you mind staying overnight? Our roads are not the best." He didn't bother to mention that they were not to be used at night; this was tacitly understood. During the day, people went about their business as best they could. Once it was dark, however, the roads were not safe for civilians. Although theirs was not a unique situation, the town, high up in the mountains, was the most remote, so Father Domingo had managed to negotiate a kind of unofficial truce that allowed his parishioners to maintain a sense of normalcy.

To his surprise, Cristina had accepted his invitation with a smile. And when he came back to town he immediately began talking to his flock about the young musician, her piano, and the pieces she would play. He drew for them a big map and he tried to explain Europe; he tried to make them imagine the kings and queens for whom this music had been written and performed. They talked about the concert after every mass from then on, until the Sunday before Cristina's arrival. And for once, those tired, dull faces lit up with excitement. Although he had anticipated an enthusiastic reaction, it was a revelation for Father Domingo: for the first time since he had arrived in this parish, the people were looking forward to something. They were happy, intrigued, but also anxious. "How should we behave? What must we say, Father?" And he had smiled and assured them they would be just fine.

"FATHER DOMINGO SENT me. My name is Federico." The man who stood at Cristina's door offered to take her bag. He had a buzzcut and a moustache, and although he was slightly shorter than her, he looked strong. He stretched out his arm and, as they shook hands, Cristina was surprised by his callous skin. It felt like sandpaper. "And...Miss, allow me to apologize for the car. It is the only one we have."

Only then did Cristina take note of the vehicle parked in front of her house. She had never seen a car so sick and severely wounded by rust. The motor was running and it seemed be suffering from a chronic cough. She remembered that Father Domingo had mentioned the roads were bad. What if the car broke down and they were left stranded in the middle of nowhere? Was it too late to cancel? She paused, considering the possibility for a minute, then thought of Father Domingo and the women and children in his town, and decided she couldn't let them down. She sighed deeply and climbed into the green jalopy, then said a little prayer that they might arrive safely in one piece.

• • •

IT TOOK EIGHT of the town's men to unload the piano from the truck.

"Who would have thought this thing would be, so heavy? Father, why didn't you invite someone with a guitar instead?" they joked as they carried the piano towards the front doors of the church. As soon as they got it inside, however, the murmur hushed. Inside the holy walls, the men became as sombre as if it were a funeral procession: the piano a huge casket, and everyone walking in silence beside it. Cástulo was still alongside Father Domingo, feeling proud.

"Here, you can leave it here." Father Domingo pointed to the open space before the altar. "Now, where is Amalia?" he asked, turning to find her. "Come here, my child. Please clean the piano with a cloth." Only then did they realize its shiny skin was covered in fingerprints. Amalia cleaned it softly, and everyone watched silently, almost in reverence. To break the tension, Father Domingo said, "Don't be afraid, it won't break!" and laughed, as everyone else did gratefully, except Amalia. She looked embarrassed and the priest felt sorry for her. He wanted to make her feel good. Especially since her husband, Trinidad, had died recently, and the baby she had been expecting was stillborn. No doctors. No rain. No help. Foreign remittances were few and far between. Only campaigning politicians brought relief, and that was mostly false hope packaged in a bag of food and coupons for free groceries. It was never enough.

"There's no hope," Amalia had said, after they buried her little baby. A boy. Amalia asked Father Domingo to baptize him before the funeral. He couldn't refuse, so Amalia dressed her infant in a white sleeper she had knitted and named him Trinidad, like his father. Then she put Trinidad in his little casket with the same care and love she would have used had he been alive.

Father Domingo had decided to give her special assignments to keep her busy. "You will be Miss Cristina's special assistant. When she arrives, you will help her with everything she needs, Amalia."

Once the piano was clean, Father Domingo opened the keyboard's lid. As he did so, he looked around. It seemed to him that the piano itself and everyone around it were smiling in unison when he held the lid open. The white keys contrasted with the people's yellowed, crooked teeth, but wood and ivory, teeth and flesh seemed happy to be together. Pedrito asked if he could touch the keys, and Father Domingo nodded. He asked the children to form a line so each of them could get a chance to play the piano. The silence that had prevailed drowned in their laughter as they discovered the different sounds the piano could make. Some of the children put their entire hand on the keys and heard a crushed sound in response. Others would touch two or three keys at a time, still not hearing a chord that made any sense. Once their turn was over, they returned to their places and fixed their eyes on the next player's fingers, trying to make a connection between what they saw and what they heard, trying to control their excitement and their laughter inside the house of God.

After the children had each had their turn, Amalia was the first grown-up to try. She approached the keyboard with fear and ran her fingers smoothly over its surface, from left to right. The sound her hand produced was like a waterfall, and those who came after her tried to imitate it, from bass to treble and back, their dirty fingernails clacking against the piano's smile, their calluses stumbling on the way up or down.

"Okay now, Cástulo, you are the last one, would you like to try? After all, it's thanks to you that we have the piano here today." Cástulo bit his lower lip and inclined his head. He didn't want Father Domingo to notice he was nervous, but his index finger fell casually on a key, high-pitched as a flame, and he lifted it immediately as if it had burned him. He was laughing, his forehead shiny.

After everyone had had a turn— "What a relief the town is small!" thought Father Domingo—Amalia cleaned the keys with a cotton ball dabbed in alcohol. She did it carefully, softly, even lovingly, and again Father Domingo thought what a wonderful mother she would have made.

It was getting late. "Back to your work, please, and be here on time this evening. The bells will ring to announce the beginning of the concert."

CRISTINA WAS ABOUT to doze off when Federico exited the highway and made a right onto a country road. They were at the foot of a mountain and about to head up.

"It looks like this area hasn't had much maintenance lately." The landscape had changed again, from scattered houses to an abundance of trees and scarce evidence of any human presence.

"We used to have rosewood and mahogany here, but now it's mostly pine and juniper trees."

"What happened?" Cristina was too embarassed to confess she was unable to tell one tree from the next.

"People from the city happened. Politicians. They know nothing about the land but feel free to distribute and legislate it as they please." Federico frowned and started to slow down. "And now, *them*." Carefully, he manoeuvred around a tree trunk lying on the road.

"Who's 'them'?" Cristina looked around, searching for people, her senses on high alert.

"Let's put it this way: certain people have taken advantage of the current deforestation to plant stuff they're not supposed to."

All the windows in the car were open and despite the heat, Cristina shivered. As they advanced higher up the mountain, she kept her eyes and ears open. Who was really in control here? Why had she agreed to come?

"If we're lucky, maybe we'll run into a white-tailed deer. We have skunks too, and coyotes. Oh! And every kind of lizard you can imagine."

Federico gave her a smile, and Cristina tried to conceal her worry by smiling back. She had always been bad at lying.

"Don't worry, Señorita. Father Domingo is very respected around here. He has kept our town out of trouble since he arrived. God knows how he's done it, but he has. Everyone knows this is his car. We're fine. The only thing to fear is fear itself—and potholes." Cristina laughed, and when Federico saw her shoulders relax a little, he let out a sigh of relief.

AMALIA HAD JUST finished cleaning the piano and sweeping the floor of the church when Cristina arrived. Father Domingo was there to meet her as she stepped out of the car.

"Oh, Father! You didn't tell me the road would be so bad. Every bone in my body aches," Cristina said, making an effort not to mention anything other than the state of the road. Would she be able to return home safely? For now, relieved to have arrived without incident, she smiled at the children who had gathered to welcome her.

"I'm sorry, my child. I thought I had mentioned it to you."

"Hi, Señorita Cristina, my name is Pedrito, and I'm very happy you're finally here," the boy said, extending his hand in the gentlest manner, as he thought would be appropriate. Now the other children were surrounding her and extending their hands, hoping to shake hers just as Pedrito had done.

"Thank you Pedrito, I'm happy too," she replied, gladly shaking all the little hands that came close to her, unable to remember the names that floated on the light voices: Pablo, Maria, Lalo, Lupita, Pepe, Tere.

Cristina took a quick survey of the town square. The street was merely insinuated, invented by the houses built on both sides of the road. The church had once been white; its paint was now peeling and dirty. The ground was dry, the sun hit it like an unforgiving drill. Cristina saw a yellow dog scratching its neck, a small, malnourished horse tied to a skinny tree, and some women walking down the street carrying heavy baskets. She heard some animal noises, although she couldn't make them out, and then she focused her attention back on Pedrito. He was maybe ten, she thought. He wore no shoes, and she marvelled at the fact that he walked easily, as if the ground wasn't hot enough to fry an egg. She felt an instant respect for him, as well as for the other children. Not even the youngest ones wore shoes. She had to make an effort not to cry, and she felt a pang of guilt over her earlier apprehension on the road.

Father Domingo led her inside the church. The air was cool but stale. The few decorations around the altar seemed almost sad, even with the piano at their feet. Cristina walked over to it, sat down on the bench, and placed her hands on the keyboard.

"I just want to check if it's properly tuned, is that all right?"

The children applauded, and she smiled. What she didn't say was that she feared the ride on the bumpy road might have ruined its sound. She played a few scales to begin with, but the children, Father Domingo, Cástulo, and even Federico were standing around her in disbelief. Was this the same piano they had been torturing a few hours ago?

Father Domingo dismissed the children before they started asking Cristina to play more. Then he introduced her to Amalia. Cristina reached out to take her hand, but Amalia shook her head and blushed. "My hands are ugly, Miss, please forgive me." Instead, Amalia took Cristina's bag into the sacristy and showed her where she could rest. The small room was full of religious decorations. There was also a bed, a night table, and a small altar. Through the window, there was nothing to see except dry empty land.

"Would you like something to eat?" Amalia offered. But Cristina said she only wanted water and a nap before the concert. The bedsheets smelled fresh and clean, and she felt so comfortable in their mild embrace that she quickly fell into a deep sleep.

When she awoke from her nap, Cristina changed into a long pink dress. She was struggling to apply her makeup with only the help of her tiny compact mirror when she was startled by heavy scraping and ponderous thuds. Something was happening outside. Her heart began to pound. Perhaps it had been a mistake to come here after all.

She left the sacristy cautiously and was relieved to find Amalia outside the door. She asked her what was going on. Amalia took a few seconds before answering; she was astonished by the pink dress and how beautiful Cristina looked in it. She wanted to touch the fabric desperately but was too shy to ask, so she hid her hands behind her back to stop the temptation.

"I'm so sorry we disturbed you," she said finally, "but while you were sleeping we decided to make some last-minute changes."

Cristina looked puzzled, so Amalia led her to the back of the altar, where they could see men carrying the church benches outside. Father Domingo approached the women and explained to Cristina what Amalia already knew:

"Our church is too poor a place for you to play. The people thought you deserved better."

"What do you mean? What are they doing?"

"They are pushing our old benches to the very back of the church."

"Yes, I can see that, Father. But why?"

"Because tonight they want this place to look beautiful. So everyone is going to bring their best chair."

It took Cristina a few seconds to understand what Father Domingo was saying.

"You mean they're going to carry chairs from their houses all the way here for the concert?"

"Yes. They will bring their nicest chairs. We decided this after you went to sleep, so now we must hurry to be ready on time."

THE BELLS TOLLED their tired sounds shortly before the sun disappeared over the horizon. People arrived on time and once everyone was seated, Father Domingo invited Cristina to come in. She was received with warm applause. As she stood in front of her audience, she couldn't help but notice the chairs, which had been arranged in neat rows. In any given row, two or three chairs looked exactly alike, then the next few appeared to be part of a different set. Some were big, some were small. Some were blue or green or yellow, or had embroidered flowers, or were just plain and discoloured. She recognized Amalia sitting in the front row, and Pedrito with his hair combed down — with lime juice, maybe? She didn't recognize any of the others really, but their hair too was either wet or combed very close against the scalp, making their heads look too big. She caught a faint whiff of soap and cheap cologne, but what she was most aware of was their eyes, which appeared to be caressing her skin like a veil.

"Tonight's program will begin with a piece called Prelude, Chorale and Fugue by César Franck. He was a nineteenth-century composer who was born in Belgium but lived in France for most of his life." Cristina was unsure if she had chosen the right words, and promised herself she would be more informal when introducing the next piece. Then she took a seat and started to play. The Prelude proved to be a breathtaking beginning. The audience absorbed every note she played into their bodies. She had chosen this piece for its religious character, thinking it would suit the church setting perfectly, but hadn't expected such a respectful atmosphere. When she glanced briefly at Father Domingo, she understood what true communion was. The applause was solemn, still a bit shy. Cristina was happy anyway. She was always happy when she played the piano.

Next she introduced Schubert's Wanderer Fantasy, explaining that the composer, who had always been very poor, died when he was only thirty-one years old. Thinking that the audience would relate to Schubert's situation, but not wanting to make them feel sad, she went on to say that he had been a genius who composed many different pieces. The one they were about to hear represented a crossing through happy and nostalgic worlds, "poetic and brilliant and dancing in its final part." She wanted them to imagine people strolling and dancing to such music, to picture what those worlds were like, their colours and their smells.

Next, Cristina said she would play some of Johannes Brahms's waltzes. She explained that the waltz was a type of dance born in Vienna, Austria, and it had caused a musical and social revolution because it was the first dance in which partners embraced each other. This was greeted by shy laughter, which was silenced immediately by Father Domingo's firm gaze.

While listening to the music, Cástulo pictured himself in a big hall, dancing with a lady in a long, elegant dress, and he smiled shyly, surprised at how much he was enjoying the music, which he would have found boring before.

All of the waltzes were brief; some ran at a quick pace, some were slow. During the second-to-last piece, Amalia shed a tear; its slow motion made her feel like cradling her baby in her arms and lulling him to sleep. She thought, maybe Trinidad was listening too, and holding their son for her at that very moment?

The applause that followed the waltzes was happy and energetic, and Cristina was very pleased to see the bright faces and hear the clapping hands telling her how much they liked what they had just heard. She realized that she and her audience were exchanging gifts of sound, bartering music and clapping. What a privilege it was for her to bring the music to these people for the first time in their lives. For the first time! During her first winter abroad as a student, she had experienced the magic of snow for the first time. She remembered walking in the cold brisk air, catching snowflakes in her hands and her mouth, walking around just for the pleasure of feeling the snow crunch under her boots. Today she was striving to give Father Domingo's flock a gift as marvellous as her first experience of snow had been. So she dedicated the last piece to the children, especially Pedrito.

"Has anyone ever seen a tarantula?" she asked the congregation.

"Yes, Miss," answered Pedrito, "and I am not afraid of them."

"Me neither, me neither," said a little girl sitting beside him, and they all laughed.

Cristina went on: "Of course you're not afraid. But there are people who are, and next you will hear a tarantella, which is a dance inspired by the way a person jumps after being bitten by a tarantula." The children clapped, grinning, and Cristina played the Tarantella and Canzona Napoletana by Franz Liszt. Pedrito sat on his knees so he could better see Cristina's fingers transform themselves into spiders' legs, crawling up and down the keyboard at an amazing pace, chasing each other and jumping like the people they had supposedly bitten. When Cristina finished playing, he was the first to get to his feet and applaud as loudly as he could. The other children joined him and formed a cheerful band. Father Domingo said *Braaavo!* and everybody echoed him. The accoustics inside the church magnified sound, and Cristina felt almost crushed by the crowd's enthusiasm.

No, she didn't want to finish either, so she played an encore.

"Polonaises were performed at weddings in Poland, a country in Eastern Europe where it gets very, very cold," she said, "until a very important composer, named Frédéric Chopin, composed polonaises with a twist, making them dramatic pieces full of patriotism, like this one called Heroic." While she played she thought about Pedrito and his toughened feet, Amalia and her intriguing shyness, the horse she was sure was no more malnourished than its owners, and the heroic jalopy that had brought her all the way here, dodging the ferocious holes in the road like a keen bullfighter.

Father Domingo looked on, grateful that the evening had ended peacefully, without unwanted interruptions.

It was yet further proof that his flock deserved better. What a privilege it was for him to be here this evening, witnessing something that was almost a miracle: the entire town inside the church, their problems momentarily forgotten as they allowed themselves to be enveloped by the music. He looked around the gathered crowd: there was Cástulo, eyes half shut, head bent, and hands resting on his knees; Federico, who had smiled when he heard that he shared Chopin's first name; Amalia, her arms around her middle, lips shaped in a peaceful smile for the first time in months; Pedrito, once more trying to sit taller in his chair and stretching his neck like a turtle in the sun; and his brothers and sisters and all the other children, quiet like statues, unbelievable models of good behaviour—even Rosario and Alfredo, who owned the only cantina in town, and whom Father Domingo seldom saw even at Sunday Mass, had shut down for the evening and were sitting at the back of the church, hand in hand on their metal chairs, listening.

Father Domingo understood why people were always so moved by this particular piece. It made you love the place where you first heard it and feel proud of your homeland, even if that homeland was moribund, like the one beneath his feet that he cared so much about. Most of all, it gave listeners hope. Looking more closely at the faces around him, he was almost sure he could see the same conclusion as it dawned in their eyes. He could almost touch their feelings. They were warm and salty, like a sea breeze. Like the tears that filled their eyes when — after applauding feverishly and yelling *Bravo!* until they could yell no more — they approached Cristina respectfully to thank her. Then they left in silence, each one carrying their own chair as they disappeared into the dry night.

Svetlana of Montreal

"NOTHING IS CRUELLER than hope." Svetlana holds her teacup in one hand and the little saucer in the other. The indigo-blue china matches her eyes, a sharp contrast to her milk-white hair — a white that reminds me of my bridal dress, which once symbolized my own hopes but is now a spectre haunting my closet. "Nothing is crueller."

Svetlana's delicacy, her restraint, is discordant with the present. It's January 4, 1998, and we are being treated to what meteorologists are already callling the worst snowstorm in a hundred years. One hundred years, one hundred winters — an entire century has never seen a day as dreadful and dangerous as today. So here we are, Svetlana and I, in her small apartment in the Plateau, chatting over tea. One hundred years out of which she's been alive for . . . how many? Eighty-something for sure. And at least the last fifty in Montreal. No one in my family has made it to eighty. Not even a distant relative. No one.

Svetlana is sitting in her armchair, her deep blue eyes fixed on mine. Had I not come to know her as well as I do, the smile on her face would trick me into believing the tale she is about to tell is a happy one. I don't dare ask her if in Kiev, where she was raised after her family left Moscow, she ever experienced a storm like this. I don't dare ask because I'm aware that being in this comfortable room during a storm is very different than being in a city occupied by a brutal enemy army and later, by an equally brutal regime. Life must have been hard even on sunny days, but Svetlana doesn't like to talk about it. She hardly mentions it. Hardly complains. Even about Ivan's death. We barely talk about it now, even though I know we both have trouble falling asleep at night — even though sometimes I'd like to talk about him non-stop. Cry non-stop. Scream non-stop. Svetlana won't open the door to my pain, so I've learned to live with it festering inside me like a dead fetus my body isn't ready to part with. Occasionally one of us will say something like *Ivan would've loved these strawberries* or *Ivan would be furious if he heard that news.* Then we nod and fall silent or change the subject to something empty and meaningless like *Pierre's café was full of tourists today.* Anything to yank us away from the moment. Anything to help us forget that Ivan is no longer here, that it will be a year in March, a year that will feel like three hundred and sixty-five storms. But today, oddly enough, we are at peace.

"I was six years old," Svetlana says, taking a sip of her tea. "Six, and I still remember every detail. I was in charge of cleaning his boots. 'Svetlana, go to the shed and scrub your father's boots clean,' yelled my mother, and I immediately did as I was told. I scrubbed them with the same brush we used for the horses. And I had to scrub really hard because they were big for my hands and the leather was drunk with blood: the large dark stains had already begun to dry. Why would you wear boots in the middle of the summer, I wanted to ask, but I knew better and kept my mouth shut. Back then, people said that children were to be seen and not heard. I was barefoot. I liked the feeling of the grass tickling my feet. The warmth of the sun. It was July."

July in Russia. I try to picture it but fail. Ivan and I were supposed to go there together. We were going to explore Svetlana's homeland side by side. Like Chekhov's characters, we dreamed of going to Moscow, but more than that, we longed to visit Kiev and look for the dacha where Svetlana used to spend her summers. Ivan had fond memories of the chalet close to Mont Tremblant she used to rent when he was younger, and he wanted to see for himself the lakes and landscapes that were trapped forever in his grandmother's black-and-white childhood photographs. It doesn't take a huge effort to see how much of the spirited girl still inhabits this old lady. Her eyes have a soul of their own.

"Mother was packing when I came running into the house," she continues. "It's not like we had much, of course. Not like people nowadays—like children nowadays. Montreal wasn't the city you see now, either, when I arrived. There were not as many shops and restaurants. People went to church on Sundays, so I did, too. I wanted to belong. And I got used to everything—except the accumulation of possessions that is the modern world's sickness."

I am about to comment on the stacks of books spilling out of her bookcases when, as if she has read my mind, she adds, "Books don't count. They're not mere objects. They are lives. Worlds." She places her teacup in the saucer on the coffee table. "And mine changed forever that day. Mother wanted to go to Paris, but Father had insisted on Kiev. He had family there, he would find a job, they spoke the language, and the distance from Moscow would keep them safe. And so it was until Stalin condemned the Ukraine to starvation, Father was incarcerated, and the Nazis arrived."

Svetlana rises to her feet and slowly, deliberately walks to the window. I don't know what she's looking at. There's nothing to see outside. Ice pellets mixed with snowflakes are hammering the glass, building a coat that will soon obstruct our view. The wind moans, the wood creaks. She told me once that wood expands and contracts according to the weather. I like to believe this is how trees remind us that they're alive and breathing. Expand, contract; expand, contract, like Svetlana's back. I don't dare fracture her silence.

"Did you know that Montreal's sister city is Hiroshima, Tazie?" She doesn't turn around to face me. "Funny, eh? A city that knows nothing about fear or pain since the floods of 1642 is twinned with the city that faced this century's worst horror. And to think that when I arrived here, I saw the cross on top of Mount Royal as a symbol of hope! I realized too late it was a warning. A grave marker. This is where we three had come to die: Irina, Ivan, and next it will be my turn."

I stand up to go to my room. I no longer feel like talking. Irina — Ivan's mother — was a drug addict, and as far as I'm concerned she brought her death upon herself. Plus, she abandoned her son to be raised by his grandmother. Ivan, *my* Ivan, deserved better.

The wood creaks beneath my feet and gives me away. Svetlana turns around and her eyes order me to sit back down. I obey, but my throat catches at the memory of my mother and my grandmother. Their eyes were always gentle.

"It's important that you listen to what I have to say," she commands, "because I never managed to say it to him. I have no one else. Do you understand?"

Svetlana used to be a literary translator. She worked alone her entire life. When I met her, she no longer had any family, and her friends and colleagues had all moved away or died. All she had then was Ivan. And now, all she has is me.

"I saw the stretcher covered in mud," she says. "I saw it, and I immediately knew."

The stretcher was covered in mud. I didn't know that the stretcher was covered in mud, although it makes sense to me now. No, on second thought, it doesn't. It makes no sense for such an accident to happen in this country. It makes no sense that they had dug trenches that collided, trapping workers under five hundred kilos of soil and concrete and that it took twenty minutes to reach them while their lives faded away. Twenty minutes. I had experimented by trying to stand on one leg for twenty minutes, and I couldn't take it. Then I tried squatting for twenty minutes. It didn't matter that I was young, my knees and muscles felt like they were on fire. I forced myself to hold my breath at intervals for twenty minutes and I thought I'd faint. Ivan was buried for twenty minutes. And today, ten months after his death, I find out that the stretcher was covered in mud! I want to scream that Montreal is full of drug addicts and builders who pay insignificant fines for breaking the building code while the city's infrastructure falls to pieces and people die. Every five days a worker dies. *Ivan* died, and no one cares and nobody remembers and life goes on, and only a storm the likes of which has never been seen gives this place the punishment it deserves. I bite my lip to stop myself from telling Svetlana what I think about her adoptive city, how profoundly I regret not going back to my homeland, with its palm trees and constant sunshine. After I finished my studies and moved in with Ivan, I believed that life would be better but it was exactly the same crap as back home only with an inhumane winter—and now, without him.

"Get us a drink," Svetlana says as she turns back to her armchair. Her tea must be getting cold. "I feel like having some vodka. It's on the balcony, behind the large flower-pot." She signals with her head for me to get it, and I must be even more desperate than I thought because I do as she says. Without bothering to put on my coat, I venture outside and push the flowerpot aside with my bare hands to reach for the bottle. Who the hell hides vodka behind a flowerpot on the balcony during a Montreal winter? I hope I won't be like this if I make it to eighty. The ice and snow pelt my head and face and make me squint. The chattering of my teeth is the only sound I can hear. The storm has muted the city. Montreal seems to be submerged in water, like Svetlana when she was a child and had to be a fish.

My fingers are numb. I think about Ivan's fingers struggling against the mud falling on him and there's nothing in the world that I need more right now than a shot of vodka.

I should have put my coat on, I'm an idiot, but at least I put on my boots. I hold the bottle in my hands like I've just found pirates' treasure.

When I scuttle back inside, my hair is coated in ice pellets and my cheeks are burning. Svetlana is waiting for me with two shot glasses and some cheese. Shaking off the snow, I hand her the bottle as if it were a trophy, and she smiles. I go back to the sofa and wrap myself in the blanket she knitted herself long ago, when Ivan had hepatitis and she had to step away from the typewriter to be at his bedside day and night.

"Do you believe in coincidences, Tazie?" She hands me the shot glass, filled to the brim with vodka. Tazie: I like how she pronounces my name, a whiplash on the *a* and then a *z* like champagne bubbles. Ivan called me Tazie. If she dies—no, *when* she dies—this sound will die, too. I wish I could carve it inside my ears. "Anastasia" never had such a captivating ring to it.

"I don't know." I take the glass and throw back the vodka in a single gulp. It shocks me awake, clears my mind, warms my body. I toast to Ivan in secret. "I don't know what I believe in anymore, Svetlana."

She swallows her drink in one shot too, and pours us another.

"I was born in Yekaterinburg. Have you heard of Yekaterinburg?"

I shake my head. I thought she was born in Moscow.

"It was easier to talk to Ivan about Moscow." Once again, she has read my mind. I understand, or at least try to, and take a little sip of vodka this time. Svetlana's eyes, always in command, tell me to drink more. I take another sip, and then I cut myself a piece of cheese. It's a smelly French cheese — no, I correct myself — *Québecois* cheese. (I've been trained well.) One of those cheeses my mother would have thrown out but that Ivan had taught me to enjoy. I have a feeling Svetlana is about to tell me all I need to know about Yekaterinburg.

"My father used to work at the Ipatiev House, Tazie. Have you heard of it?"

I shake my head again. I'm beginning to feel a bit light-headed, but at least the cheese is good.

"We lived on the outskirts of the grounds of the Ipatiev House. It belonged to a mining engineer before the revolution. Nicholas and Alexandra and their children were held captive there for seventy-eight days before they were executed. Did you know that?"

I shake my head once more. I had never associated Svetlana with the tsars. I pour myself another shot.

"The day Father arrived home with his boots soaked in blood, the day my mother was frantically packing for us to flee Yekaterinburg, was the day they killed the Romanovs. July 17, 1918. Almost eighty years have passed and I remember every detail of that day as if it were yesterday. I tried to clean Father's boots but the blood wouldn't come out. We had to leave them behind. They were good boots, made of fine leather." She pours herself another vodka. "We left as soon as it was dark. Mother was crying. I didn't understand what was going on until many years later, after they released Father from jail. I had just turned twenty-nine. The Nazis arrived in Kiev that year. Father lost forty kilograms while he was incarcerated. He became his own ghost. They destroyed his stomach. Couldn't retain any food. They set him free so he would starve to death in front of his family."

I feel like I should say something but my mind is blank. All of this is so foreign to me. But this is Ivan's grandmother and I was going to be Ivan's wife, so I force myself to pay attention, even though I can tell that what she is going to say next will be painful.

"Father told me everything before he died. He wanted someone to remember. 'They made me kill them,' he said. 'The girls, Alexei.' He described how the Bolsheviks had improvised a firing squad and forced him to shoot. My father, the man who had been in charge of bringing the Romanov family their food, who had heard the girls sing and Alexei recite poetry. He, who had a little girl at home. According to him, the first ones to fall were the parents. Most of the bullets were aimed at Nicholas and Alexandra because nobody wanted to shoot the children. They were crying. Screaming. Terrified and wounded, but alive. Olga, Maria, and Anastasia pleaded, but when they shot them they did not die. They did not die. So the men were forced to stab Alexei and the girls with bayonets—they sliced their throats as if they were animals. It took them more than twenty minutes to die. Twenty minutes of cries and pleas and screams. Twenty minutes of children dying. Children that my father had fed."

All of a sudden I feel close to those people I had never thought of before. Their suffering is a punch in my stomach. I can picture them covered in blood, their desperate voices begging for mercy. For twenty minutes. Like Ivan.

"Do you know why they didn't die?" Svetlana downs another shot of vodka. "Because they had sewn so many diamonds into their undergarments that the bullets couldn't penetrate. And they sewed those diamonds there because they believed they still had a future. So you see how I'm right? Nothing's crueller than hope."

I don't know what to say, so I drink. I promise myself this will be the last shot. My hands are sweating and the pulse in my temples is in a crescendo. I need to lie down.

"Father got to keep some of those diamonds. He hid them from both my mother and me. He felt guilty, he said. Didn't want to use them or sell them, can you believe that? He allowed us to go hungry while those precious stones were hidden out of sight somewhere. When he went to jail, he thought he deserved it, not for opposing the Soviet regime but for what he had done during the revolution." Svetlana's fists are clenched now. "He gave me the diamonds shortly before he died. Thanks to them, I made it to Montreal, purchased this apartment, established myself here. I was going to give them to Irina as a wedding present, but you know, her sickness. . . . Money would have only accelerated her death. I never told her about them."

I want to go to my room. I don't want to listen anymore. But Svetlana stretches her arm out and stops me.

"Do you believe in coincidences, Anastasia? As soon as I learned your name, I had a ring made especially for you. I planned to give it to Ivan so that it could be his wedding present to you."

I look at her and feel as if my entire body is shattering. I don't want any ring, I want Ivan! I don't want to be in this city, and I don't want to think about mudslides or murdered children. I'm not as strong as she is. Svetlana puts her hand into her pocket and takes out a ring. She places it on the coffee table and, without making any further eye contact, gets up and heads towards her bedroom.

"Nothing's crueller than hope." Her voice lingers in the air and I set my gaze on her hunched back. She stops for an instant before opening her door: inhale, exhale. *Nothing's crueller than hope*, I repeat to myself, and remember an experiment I read about where scientists put a mouse in a bucket full of water and just before it drowned they allowed it to hold on to something for a moment. Then, they put it back in the water and the mouse swam and swam and swam far longer than all the other mice they experimented with because it had saved itself once and the hope of doing so again kept it going. But hope didn't save it; it only prolonged its agony.

Svetlana closes her door and leaves me on my own in the living room. It's getting dark outside and the snow is falling like it wants to erase the world. I stare at the ring and pray that it does. I pray that it does.

Kamp Westerbork

I WAS ABOUT to ask Mother to stop packing so we could take a walk before sunset—I knew how much she enjoyed Ottawa's crisp air in the spring—when she turned silent and her face darkened. She had hummed most of the afternoon away as we went through Grandfather's belongings, deciding which items we would keep and which we would donate or throw away. Humming was what she did when she was upset and trying to fight back tears, something her father had taught her when she was a little girl. "Don't give anyone power over you by showing weakness," he had said. "Always show strength, even at the worst of times." These words had gotten him through the war. And so she hummed, which made me think of her as two people in one: A grown-up who, from time to time, did what was necessary to calm down the fussy, scared, sad, or angry baby that lived inside her. A baby that was never allowed to cry.

"Are you okay?" Her sudden silence made it seem like the room was shrouded by a veil. There were boxes, clothes, shoes, books, and magazines everywhere. We had started a donation pile by the window, a keeping pile on the couch, and a garbage pile next to the front door of the apartment. Grandfather's medals were resting next to Mother's purse. We had already removed the pictures from the walls without dusting the tops of the frames, and assigned them to appropriate piles. The discolouration of the empty spaces where they had hung made me think of Grandfather — like his framed photographs and paintings, he was no longer there, but he had left such a clear mark that even in his absence he was present. It didn't feel right to be there, going through his belongings, opening drawers that he would have never allowed me to open. I would have much preferred to go back to Toronto after the funeral instead of staying behind to help settle his affairs, but Mother needed my company and support, and I felt obliged to be there. Her relationship with her father had not always been the best, and doing this alone would have been terribly painful for her. So there I was, watching her lose herself in an open book she held in her hands. From its pages she extracted a yellowed card, which she examined before handing it to me to read.

Lager Westerbork. Ausweiskarte
Name: Reyes Hagenaar
Vorname: Maryka Antonia
Geboren: 5.3.1900

"I don't understand." I stretched out my arm to give her back the card. "What is this?"

"An identity card."

That much I had been able to infer, but Grandfather's name was not on it.

"Who does it belong to?"

"A woman he met at Westerbork."

Of course I had heard the story of Grandfather's regiment liberating the transit camp where the Nazis held Dutch Jews until they were ready to be deported to the East. He wasn't fond of talking about what he had seen during his days as a soldier, but he was proud of his part in helping over eight hundred prisoners who were still at Kamp Westerbork on April 12, 1945, when the Canadian forces arrived. Anne Frank herself had been at Westerbork until the previous September, and when Grandfather presented me with her diary the day I turned thirteen, he wrote inside that he wished they had arrived at the camp earlier and been able to save her. Until his death, Grandfather marked each April 12th by going to church and lighting a candle. Before passing away, he made Mother promise she would continue the tradition for him.

"There were over eight hundred prisoners at Westerbork. What was special about this one that he kept her identity card?" I asked. Mother was now holding a pressed flower in her hand. "And why did he never talk about her?"

"He did." She placed the flower back between the pages of the book and passed it to me. *Twenty Love Poems and a Song of Despair* by Pablo Neruda. I had never seen the book in Grandfather's house before. I always assumed he wasn't the kind of man who liked poetry.

"He did?" I was genuinely intrigued. "Who was she?"

"Take a look at the flower."

I obliged. It was discoloured, but I could tell it had once been purple.

"What kind of flower is it?" I don't know why I brought it close to my nose; if it had ever had any scent, it had evidently lost it long ago.

"It's a mallow."

I shrugged, still not grasping what she was trying to say.

"A Malva."

"That's our name!" I was trying to put two and two together, but nothing made sense. "Can you please explain?"

Mother nodded and asked me to sit by her side. She explained that Maryka was one of the first prisoners Grandfather met after entering the camp, one of the first to come walking out of the barracks, slowly, in fear. The Nazis had fled, but the prisoners left behind were afraid they would return, so they hid when they heard tanks approaching. The Canadian soldiers arrived at what appeared, at first glance, to be an empty, silent place. But little by little, as the minutes went by, people started coming out of their hiding spots in the barracks and approaching their liberators.

After the initial commotion, help was offered to those who needed immediate assistance. Maryka had been working at the camp's infirmary and was able to explain what life at Westerbork had been like. Originally built as a refugee centre for Jews fleeing persecution in Germany, Westerbork had remained under Dutch management until 1942, when it became an SS-controlled transit camp. Jews who turned themselves in or were captured in the Netherlands were sent to Westerbork, from which every Tuesday, cattle-wagon trains filled with prisoners were sent to extermination camps like Auschwitz, Sobibor, and Bergen-Belsen. Because Auschwitz had been liberated earlier that year, and word had travelled fast about the atrocities uncovered by the Russians, Grandfather was surprised when Maryka informed him that Westerbork had had a cabaret, an orchestra that gave weekly concerts, and even a school. Prisoners were allowed to wear civilian clothes as long as their yellow Star of David was visible.

At Westerbork, in spite of heavy surveillance and regular deportations, inmates experienced better conditions than those at most other camps. Maryka wore a coat that looked big on her, but her hair was combed and, even under the circumstances, it was evident she was an attractive woman. She was not Jewish, but a Dutch citizen born in Java.

I asked Mother to pause for a moment.

"Java? Why would anyone leave Java in the middle of World War II and move to the Netherlands?"

"She told Father that her husband was Chilean. She arrived in the Netherlands with him."

A Chilean in the company of a Javanese in Nazi-occupied territory. The story was getting more interesting by the minute. I couldn't believe no one had told me any of this before.

"Maryka accepted the bar of chocolate Father offered her, and by the end of the night..." I could sense that Mother was uncomfortable. Grandfather was not married to Grandmother at the time, but they were engaged. "They got cozy enough with each other for Maryka to share her entire story with him."

"And he told it to you?"

"No. I overheard it during his fights with Mother. It came up again and again. Mother was very jealous of Maryka because when Father was drunk, he always said that she was the most beautiful woman he had ever met."

"But she must have been twenty years older than him!"

"I know. Such an age difference was unusual at the time."

"Grandmother was so good-looking. It's hard to imagine her being jealous of a woman twice her age. Especially of someone Grandfather met as a soldier."

Had this Maryka been the reason my grandparents slept in separate rooms? The reason Mother had no siblings? I didn't have the courage to ask. Grandfather had mellowed by the time I was born, but I knew enough about the resentment, the yelling, the violence that Mother had dealt with growing up.

A bank employee in Java at the time she met her husband, Maryka had left the comforts of home and everything she knew to follow him to South America. Living in Santiago and Buenos Aires, she learned Spanish while he spent the evenings drinking. Maryka thought that a child might make him change his ways. She was pregnant when they moved to Madrid, where her husband worked for the Chilean government and pursued some writing projects. Maryka gave birth to a daughter, who was soon diagnosed with hydrocephalus.

"In his writing, her husband called the child 'a perfectly ridiculous being, a kind of semicolon, a three-kilo vampire.'" Mother gave a bitter smile and paused. "He actually wrote that down."

I shook my head in disbelief. I was aware that in years past little consideration had been given to children born with abnormalities, but comparing a little girl's large head and scrawny body to a semicolon seemed unusually cruel, especially for a father.

"And then he abandoned them both, right at the start of the war."

Now the relationship made more sense to me. Grandfather had also been abandoned as a child. His mother had raised him alone. No wonder he felt such empathy for Maryka and her daughter.

Leaving your family at any point in time seemed devastating and unacceptable to me, but doing so at the start of a war was unforgivable. Mother went on to explain that Maryka's husband had promised to send money but never did. Maryka was forced to leave her daughter in the care of a generous couple she met through church; it was impossible to work and tend to the child's needs at the same time. She was able to visit her only once a month because the train fare from The Hague to Gouda was a great expense.

"And she wasn't there when the girl died." Mother's eyes were aimed at the floor. I didn't know what to say. It was certainly a very sad story. "Maryka sent her husband a telegram informing him of their child's death. She received no answer. She asked him to help her leave Europe and join him wherever he happened to be living. Still no answer. She was on a train to Gouda to tend her daughter's grave when she was arrested and brought to the camp."

"Perhaps Maryka's husband didn't answer because he was dead."

"That's what your grandfather thought. But she insisted

on sending him another message. And guess who was chosen as the messenger."

"Grandfather?"

"He told me that she addressed her husband as 'My dear Pig.'"

"Lovely."

"You get the idea. So your grandfather mailed her letter, putting his own name and address on the envelope because Maryka thought her husband wouldn't open it if her name was on it."

"Did he receive an answer? Did he stay in touch with Maryka?"

"No and no. His regiment had to continue fighting. Besides, he was engaged and she was married. When the war ended he came home, married your grandmother, and put everything that had happened in Europe behind him. Or at least he tried to."

I knew what she meant. Mother had told me about the nightmares that used to make Grandfather wake up in the middle of the night, screaming, especially when she was a little girl.

"Well, thanks for sharing this piece of family history with me, I guess." I was about to stand up and continue packing, but Mother held me back.

"I'm not done."

I tilted my head. Not done? I had already heard enough.

It was getting late and we had work to finish.

"When I was born, your grandfather wanted to name me Maryka, but your grandmother refused."

"Understandable." I was beginning to lose my patience.

"So he named me Malva instead. Like Maryka's daughter. Except your grandmother didn't know that until after the fact. She never forgave him for it."

My eyes opened wide. Years before, Mother had told me an entirely different story when I had asked about our name.

"Malva was the name of Pablo Neruda's daughter." She handed me the copy of *Twenty Love Poems and a Song of Despair*. "You should keep this."

It took me a moment to absorb what I'd just heard.

"Maryka was Pablo Neruda's wife?"

Mother rolled her eyes.

"The first of three, yes."

I leafed through the book in wonder. Perhaps Grandfather had placed Maryka's identity card and a mallow flower between the pages of the first English edition of Neruda's book as his own little way of helping her. His own little way of putting a broken family back together.

I placed the book at the top of the keeping pile and looked out the window. "It's almost nighttime, Mother. I need some fresh air." I stretched out my arm, hoping she would take my hand. "Are you still up for a walk? I'd like to see the tulips."

The Last Piano

I DON'T PLAY the piano. So what? I made myself forget
how to read the notes on a staff a long time ago. I never
really cared. Aunt Diana commented bitterly on the matter
as often as she could. "With those big hands, Federica, you
could have been a great virtuoso like me," she'd say. It was
true, my hands looked like hers: long agile fingers, thin
but strong. "Ideal for sliding across the keys." "Or sliding under a pair of pants," I'd respond. She'd get furious
with me, unable to understand my teenage impulses, or
she pretended she couldn't understand them. Underneath
her perpetual smile — which few people seemed to recognize, like I did, as fake — she was imperturbable and frigid.
(Except, of course, when it came to her music.) She always
wore her hair short. In fact, she'd kept the same hairstyle for
years, almost as if she wanted to stop time from affecting

her, so that she could remain like the time-honoured music she played at her concerts. Now I realize that she wanted me to be alone too, like her, with her. That's why she wouldn't let me be.

It took me a while to get used to living with her. The first thing I learned when I arrived at her home was that the piano was more important than anyone or anything. Time allotted for practice was sacred. Nobody dared interrupt her. If she heard any other sound as she caressed the keys, that perpetual smile, that vile and ever-present sweetness she had about her, would suddenly disappear and she would stay upset for a long time. The warm-up exercises were torture, those same notes again and again: *dah-dah-dah-dah-dah-dah-dah-dah-dah*. For the longest time, when I closed my eyes I could still hear them. If I was distracted, I would find myself humming the notes; they knocked without mercy and I couldn't stop them from entering. Same scales, same hairstyle, same perfume for years. Aunt Diana was more like a replica of herself, a slightly aged copy of her teenage pictures, than a living being. And our life together was a succession of monotonous days, cold silences, and very few laughs.

I'll admit that in the beginning I wanted to be like her. I would sit at her grand piano, pounding at the keys, trying to compose a melody, my back straight and my arms extended. I couldn't yet reach the pedals. One afternoon Aunt Diana sat down beside me and began to teach me some chords. If I had known how things were going to turn out, I wouldn't have been so enthusiastic. But it didn't happen that way. I let her continue, fascinated by the feeling of her hand over mine as it slid across the fine ivory keyboard.

The next morning I was subjected to two hours of piano class. I quickly learned that confronting a scale first thing after breakfast can be nauseating. The pressure of those strange hands covering my fingers on the black and white keys, the unreadable symbols, the clefs and fractions on the paper, were enough to kill any ambition I might have had of becoming a pianist. But Aunt Diana insisted. My only release was when she played a local concert or went away on tour. Every morning and later every afternoon, she became a soft-voiced, stiff, and rigid tyrant, unyielding and uncompromising. My classes were the focal point of a routine that she wouldn't let me break. True, on Saturdays and Sundays she was a little more flexible: while she was doing yoga, she let me watch television. But after that it was back to the piano. In her interviews or among friends, she didn't hesitate to mention my progress, which she grossly exaggerated, so the question that followed was obviously whether I too wanted to become a concert pianist. Aunt Diana's threatening gaze would quash any possibility of my telling the truth. "Yes," I always responded with a beaming grin. Like aunt, like niece.

I started getting sick regularly: flus, allergies, stomach aches; and later, recurring nightmares that made my nights almost as insufferable as my days.

"Your Aunt Diana is a saint," people would tell me. I knew they meant she was a saint because she had taken me in after my parents' death — as if I needed a reminder of how my loss made her look good in other people's eyes. But after a while, her icy smile, her soft manners, her inability to recognize her own selfishness began to infuriate me. By the time I reached my teens I understood that the piano was a black hole that had sucked away my aunt's spirit — the great creator of vacuum, the gargantuan proof of my failure to meet my only family member's expectations. Another perpetual fake smile in the house.

I knew I had to prevent the piano from sucking my soul in as well.

The last year I lived with Aunt Diana, I made it a point to lock my bedroom door every night. I hated it when she touched me because it was obvious that she didn't do it with the same love with which she caressed the piano. But I had nowhere else to go. If Aunt Diana and I were vessels in a storm, the piano was her anchor. I had nothing, and I resented her all the more for that.

I tried running away a few times. I was tired of my name (what the hell did my aunt's favourite composer have to do with me, anyway?), tired of her house, her face, and her music that never changed. But I always found myself back at her door. The doorbell (Aunt Diana hated the sound of buzzers) was shaped like a small ceramic cat. The cat had caught my attention the first time I came to her house. And for a long time after, I would contemplate it happily while working up the courage to let the servants know I had returned.

Aunt Diana had wanted us to play a duet on stage, but I refused. After that, whenever she talked about me it was to complain, and people would look at me with disapproval. Diana found it easy to skew things in her favour: with her sweet expression and her soft little voice, she made it impossible for people to imagine she could do anyone any harm.

I finally left shortly before I turned nineteen. I sent her a few birthday cards but she didn't respond. Once I was on my own, I got a job working in a library. The silence and the casual conversation with the people who came looking for a book were a heavenly escape. I must say I never really missed Aunt Diana herself, except around the holidays, especially in the first few years. But then I made it a point not to think about her so much. I was determined not to live anywhere near a piano, yet her music was still locked up inside my head. I began drinking tequila to try to calm my nerves. It didn't work.

The day I finally called to speak to her (after reading about her illness in the paper and drinking half a bottle of tequila to work up the courage), I was told she couldn't come to the phone.

It wasn't easy for me to go back to the ceramic cat. I stood there a long time, biding my time before I finally rang the bell.

The maid who answered the door didn't know me, so I had to explain who I was and even show her my ID. I sported the brightest smile I could summon. Solitude sharpens the senses; I knew I had to be polite.

When I entered my aunt's room, the nurse sitting by her bed barely nodded at me. Aunt Diana, on the other hand, stretched out her arms towards me. The shock paralyzed me: she hadn't changed a bit. Her face and her hair were exactly the same. I stood by the foot of the bed and looked her over, but as hard as I tried I couldn't find anything different about her other than the dark shadows under her hazel eyes. I felt an urge to leave, yet I didn't have the courage. I took her hand and sat at the edge of the bed. She couldn't speak and her breathing came very slowly. She fell asleep with her hands between mine. I counted four seconds between each breath, and a moan every now and then.

I stayed with her for two full days and nights. I revelled in the silence around me, and the softness of her breathing. I imagined that was what it must be like to watch over a sleeping infant. It was then I decided I wanted to be a mother one day. I had never felt such peace.

Early in the morning of the third day, I noticed her breathing becoming more laboured. One…two…three…four… five…six…seven…eight seconds until her next breath, and now she didn't even have the strength to moan. I didn't warn the nurse about the change; instead I asked her to leave us alone. I curled up beside my aunt and put my hand on her chest. I could barely feel her heartbeat. I smoothed her hair and arranged it carefully so that she would look as nice as possible, and I wiped the sweat off her brow with the sleeve of my shirt. I had always envied her turned-up nose and the next-to-invisible pores on her perfect skin. She was beautiful even then. I wanted to cry, but I chose not to make a scene. We'd had enough of those already.

As her breathing became even slower, she frowned. She was in pain. Real pain. I wouldn't be able to live with myself if I let her suffer. If I called the nurse, she would only prolong the agony. I couldn't allow that. It was my last chance to show Aunt Diana that she had been wrong about me all this time. I confirmed, at that very moment, how different I was from her. I was going to set her free.

I slid my fingers slowly up towards her neck and squeezed it a bit, softly at first, but then I applied more pressure. She opened her eyes and stared at me. I hadn't expected this, and I couldn't stand it. Why was she suddenly awake? What would happen if she lived? It seemed as if she wanted to tell me something, but it was too late: the decision had been made. With my big hands, useless until that moment, I circled her neck and made a brace that helped her sleep in peace.

It wasn't easy to dismiss both the servants and the nurse. I knew they wouldn't be gone long, so I had to hurry. I didn't want the earth to swallow Aunt Diana in a cold, gloomy box when we had a much better one at home. I convinced myself that it would be unfair to separate her from the one thing she loved the most.

I didn't want to waste time changing her clothes. I simply pulled her by the ankles to get her off the bed, then dragged her to the hallway. I hadn't imagined she would be so heavy — she always watched what she ate in order to remain slim. The most difficult part was the stairs. Every time her head hit a step, the hollow sound made me shudder. I opened the door to the living room and turned on the lights. The ornaments and the paintings on the walls were the same as when I had lived there. Aunt Diana had managed to arrest time for her surroundings as well as for her skin. I still don't understand why the sun hadn't faded the upholstery or the cheerful reds and oranges in the carpet.

I opened the lid of the piano and ran my fingers over its ivory teeth as if searching for a melody that was lost in my memory. Grateful that Aunt Diana couldn't hear, I pounded the keys over and over again. Then I turned towards her.

Eyes closed and hair tousled, she lay on the marble floor of the foyer. The most important part of the plan was still to come.

Once she was lying inside the piano, I cut off her nightgown; I didn't want there to be anything between the materials of the piano and her skin and bones. She looked younger than me, more lovely than ever. But there was something missing. I went upstairs to get her perfume, and as I did I couldn't help but notice the trail of blood. I tiptoed around it, fetched the perfume bottle, tiptoed back downstairs to the living room, and anointed her: her temples, her bruised neck, her chest, her small waist, and her legs.

The smell of alcohol, gasoline, and tequila soon filled the room. The time had come to bring my most recurrent nightmare to life — and bring some heat back to Aunt Diana Guadalupe's body. After all, saints didn't deserve to feel cold, or to be buried in darkness. The piano had to melt with her and disappear from my life once and for all. It didn't matter if somebody came in now: the piano and Aunt Diana were one, and neither water nor man could separate them. The crackling of burning wood, the smell of singed hair, charred skin, and acrid smoke filled the room. As the flames grew, the sound of the scales that had tortured me, the notes that had banged on the back of my neck without mercy every day I had passed without Diana, began to fade away. For the first time I was at peace.

. . .

YES, WATER WOULD be nice. I feel like I swallowed the sun.
I have nothing more to add for now, officer, but I have
a question: Do you know if the ceramic cat survived? If so,
may I please keep it?

The Audition

"TWO THOUSAND DOLLARS?"

Behind his thick glasses, Licenciado Héctor López Méndez nodded without the slightest hint of a smile.

Two thousand dollars! How much was that in bolívares? Genesis had always been good with numbers—a perk of learning to read music before words, Tía Conchita used to say. A quick mental estimate revealed a horrifyingly high number: around twenty thousand bolívares, give or take a few. Considering the four hundred Genesis earned a month, plus whatever she could make on the side, it would take her nearly four years to gather that much money, and only if she saved all of her income. Not feasible.

Genesis struggled to keep her composure. She had chosen a blue pencil skirt for the occasion, high heels, and a white blouse which she now regretted because it would do a miserable job of hiding the sweat she could feel building up under her arms. She had assumed the air conditioning of the Servicio Administrativo de Identificación, Migración y Extranjería—or SAIME, as everyone called it—would be working and had actually been looking forward to the reprieve from the summer heat. But to her surprise, when she stepped inside the building she discovered that the employees had been forced to improvise the cooling, like everyone else in those days, and were using electric fans they had probably brought from their own homes.

The air was thick and muggy, and Genesis felt as if she was breathing through a hood. If only she could stand up and stretch her legs a little! (She always did her best thinking when she was moving.) But there was no room to pace inside that government office, which, like everything else in the country, had seen better days. The only object in the room that hinted that it was from the twenty-first century was the outdated desktop computer on which Licenciado López Méndez was reading her file. The desk, made of metal and formica laminate, was large and cumbersome, the way office furniture used to be in the 80s, and she was sitting on one of two pleather chairs facing the director of documentation issuance, her thighs and bottom already feeling sticky. Would her skirt show an embarrassing sweat stain when she stood up? She should've done a better job of choosing her outfit; she didn't need this added stress.

The one advantage of Licenciado López Méndez's office that Genesis could see was that it was on a high floor and had a privileged view of Mount Avila, majestic and green, which crowned a city that, to Genesis's mind, had lost its gloss. Caracas was like one of those 1960s Mercedes Benz she saw on the streets every so often: still running because it was well-built, but showing the wear and tear of decades without maintenance or care. In her neighbourhood, the sidewalks were cracked and the roads had potholes. It was small consolation that she could marvel at the way nature fought its way through the decay, spawning wild, colourful flowers that grew stubbornly between cracks in the pavement. The land was fertile and generous, yet gone were the bonanza days when citizens would hop on a plane to Miami to do their grocery shopping. Gone, too, the days of cavalier spending and partying, of imported Scotch served on-the-rocks and stirred with index fingers. But Mount Avila was still there, beautiful as ever. How long had it been since Genesis had taken its aerial tramway? So long ago that she couldn't even remember.

Two thousand dollars. Licenciado López Méndez might just as well have said a million; to Genesis it was equally out of reach. She had some savings, of course, and the money that Tía Conchita, her beloved aunt, had left her. She had planned to use that money to move to France to live with Angelique, her only cousin, like they had both dreamed of. But she had already been forced to use part of it just to survive. Scarcity had driven prices through the roof. Her middle-class upbringing hadn't prepared Genesis for the high cost of being poor.

Yet here she was, sitting in front of Licenciado Héctor López Méndez, an influential man who had granted her an appointment because she was a violinist in the symphony and he had been a student of Tía Conchita ages ago, in what seemed like another lifetime, a time when the arts mattered and the population had not yet been divided into predators and prey. Or had it been so different then? Genesis remembered when Tía Conchita had been mugged and so violently assaulted that she was hospitalized for a week. It wasn't enough for the thieves to steal her purse; they had pushed her around and kicked her before running away. Two young men, Tía Conchita recalled, trembling, no more than twenty years old. That should've been her wake-up call. Even Angelique had urged them to leave after that, to finally move to Perpignan to be with her. But as much as Tía Conchita dreamed of France, she didn't want to leave her home. What would happen to Roberto, her parrot, if she left? Who would take care of him? He needed a special diet, wasn't used to being alone, and enjoyed listening to music. Who would give him all that in her absence? Besides, she loved her apartment, her piano, the warm weather, the fresh *arepas* in the morning, her gentle routine as a retired

music teacher. Attending Mass on Sundays and then stopping at her favourite bakery, Tivoli, to buy a *montañita de
chocolate*—a pastry crowned with a mound of chocolate
cream, which she'd eat with delight while telling Genesis
stories of her childhood. A time when people in Caracas
didn't have to be afraid to go about their business on the
streets, when they didn't have to carry a hundred bolívares
para los ladrones—mugger money—in their purses to
appease the greedy thieves who showed no mercy when
their chosen victim had nothing to give.

If only they had stopped the urban violence and the
corruption then and there, back in the 80s, Tía Cochita
often lamented. But no, everyone had been hypnotized by
the mirage of the nation's oil wealth, thinking it would
last forever, and enjoyed the many luxuries it afforded the
lucky few: butter imported from Denmark, leather belts
and purses from Italy, shopping malls, plastic surgery, Miss
Universe titles. Was there anything they couldn't have back
then? Hindsight is 20/20, Genesis thought.

"You should move to Perpignan with Angelique,
Genesis." Tía Conchita had spoken with honesty and determination, despite her broken ribs and arm.

"I could never leave you, don't be silly. Besides, who will
take care of Roberto if I leave and you're bedridden? As you
always said, 'All for one, one for all,' right?" Tía Conchita
had made a joke about how the three of them were the

tropical version of the Three Musketeers: her, Genesis, and Roberto. In Genesis's mind, however, the third member of the trio was her violin. "'All for one, one for all,' right?"

How she had regretted her decision! She should've urged Tía Conchita to leave. One of Tía Conchita's wealthy students could have adopted Roberto, and they would have been free to go. She should have known that a country where an old lady can be mugged and kicked on the street while the police — or anyone else, for that matter — did nothing was not a country worth staying in. She should have been more alarmed that the Venezuela where she had been raised, peaceful and buoyant, had become a place where agitation and disaffection no longer simmered below the surface. She should have insisted that they pack their suitcases and leave while her passport was still valid. Or at least while it was still possible to obtain a passport that didn't cost two thousand dollars.

"Two thousand dollars?" She pronounced the words slowly to make sure she had heard them correctly.

She noticed the ring on Licenciado López Méndez's left hand. He was married. Genesis allowed herself to relax a little. Perhaps her apprehension, the discomfort that had been brewing in her stomach, was uncalled for. Perhaps she would be able to keep the gold chain with the treble clef charm after all. She had brought it along just in case. It had been a gift from Tía Conchita after Genesis's first recital. Eighteen-karat gold, the norm in those days. *Los bienes son para remediar los males*, she had told herself as she secured the small piece of jewelry to her bra with a pin. You can fight some evils with goods. Material goods. She was willing to give it a shot but secretly hoped it wouldn't come to that. Licenciado López Méndez had been a boy once, a student of Tía Conchita's. She would try to appeal to that memory first.

"Señorita Genesis, I'm sure you understand the current circumstances. There are simply too many requests for passports and other identification papers for me to tell you if they will be approved and when they will be ready, unless something is done to expedite the process."

She knew what he was talking about. Lineups had become a part of daily life in Caracas. It didn't matter where you went or what services you asked for: you had to stand in line. How many people had she read about who collapsed under the heat of the sun while they waited? She had dreaded the lineup surrounding this building. She had seen men and women of all ages carrying children, even babies, standing in a disorderly line talking to one another. Some of them held up umbrellas for protection against the sun. Others complained that they had arrived at dawn yet had only moved forward a few metres. Someone said he had heard they could only serve four hundred people a day, and there were way more than that many waiting in line now;

should they leave and try again the next day? One woman said she had been coming every day for a week without any luck; she was in tears because without the new mandatory ID she couldn't buy groceries on the assigned day.

Swallowing her guilt over jumping the queue and not waiting outside with everyone else, Genesis had walked slowly past the crowd so as not to attract attention. Once she reached the front of the line, she boldly stated that she had an appointment with Licenciado Héctor López Méndez and walked into the building and towards the elevator. No questions were asked. Several days ago she had submitted her application and all her documents online through the portal as required, but that was not enough. She knew that without this man's help she would get nowhere.

"Licenciado López Méndez," she said, looking him in the eye. He was short and plump, and his Bratwurst fingers held on to a wrinkled handkerchief that he used to wipe the sweat from his face and neck. "Licenciado López Méndez, you are a cultured man. My aunt always spoke highly of you. She said you had a talent for music." She hoped he wouldn't be able to tell she was lying. "Perhaps if you knew the reason for my urgency you would understand the kind of pressure I am under and would look kindly on my situation."

Genesis told him she had been offered an audition with an orchestra abroad. Not in France, unfortunately, not in

Perpignan—in case he remembered Tía Conchita's dreams and musings—but in Toronto, Canada. It was the opportunity of a lifetime.

"It's a blind audition. I have to be there in person and play behind a screen. That's how it's done there."

She had to cover her own airfare and expenses, which was already going to be difficult for her. And although she knew that the likelihood of being hired was low (she added this, trying to appear humble), she wanted this experience so that she could bring the knowledge she gained home to Caracas. What she didn't mention was plan B: to claim asylum in Canada and, if that didn't work, to reach out to Angelique in Perpignan. She hadn't worked out all the details yet. She needed a passport first.

"Is it possible to . . . to find another way? I can't afford two thousand dollars, much less in cash." Genesis had promised herself she would appear objective and professional at this meeting, but her trembling voice betrayed her. Cash! Bolívares were so worthless now that Venezuelan migrants were weaving purses out of hundred-dollar bills to sell on the streets of Bogotá and Quito. People had to carry mountains of money with them to pay for everyday needs. Two thousand dollars in bolívares would fill a suitcase or two, no doubt. And walking down the street with two thousand US dollars in cash seemed like a suicide mission, especially for an unescorted woman.

Two. Thousand. Dollars. What could she sell to raise that much money? How much could her television, her laptop, her microwave, and the dresses she wore on stage be worth? The washing machine had already been sold. She knew she would eventually be going away and she didn't want to leave anything valuable behind. The people who had lived in her apartment building the longest, the ones who had been there from the beginning, like Tía Conchita, were already gone. They had either died or emigrated. Half the people she knew were either in Miami or Panamá. They had fled the country by airplane, car, bus, even by foot. Carmelita, who had been the superintendent since before Genesis moved in with Tía Conchita to study music, had packed her most vital belongings in a suitcase and hopped a bus to the Colombian border, where she intended to continue her journey on foot until she reached her sister in Bucaramanga.

"If we stay, we'll starve," she had said. "You should leave before things get worse and it's too late." Carmelita had given her good advice. But Genesis couldn't abandon Tía Conchita. Who would take care of her?

Take care of her. How naïve! It was impossible to take care of anyone in a country that was falling apart. The scarcity of food and medicine at the peak of the crisis made it impossible. Tía Conchita's health was declining fast. She had fallen twice and become incontinent. Genesis's colleagues at the symphony helped her find the right connections to purchase absorbent pads, but they were almost never the right size, and there were not enough of them. She had to improvise by cutting up tablecloths, bedsheets, and towels. When there was a water shortage, the stench in the apartment became unbearable. Genesis still had to attend rehearsals and pretend that everything was fine; she knew better than to criticize the government or complain about her hardships when others were going through worse. Tía Conchita, who had always been strong and confident, an independent woman who prided herself on never needing a man by her side, could no longer look Genesis in the eye.

"Señorita Genesis, I hold your aunt in great esteem. That's why I agreed to see you. But you must understand that the situation is very hard for everybody." Licenciado Héctor López Méndez was folding his wrinkled wet handkerchief.

Hard for everybody? Not for someone like him, Genesis imagined. A man with a government position that entitled him to demand a two-thousand-dollar bribe in exchange for granting a document that she had the legal right to request and cost a fraction of that amount to produce. When was the last time this dirtbag had felt hungry? she wondered. At the peak of the crisis it had been hard for people to find food for themselves, let alone for their pets. Roberto had gone without his special seeds for a few days, and Genesis knew—because Tía Conchita had warned her—that if he ate anything other than those seeds he would die. Fucking parrot, she thought, but nevertheless she searched every pet store downtown for those special seeds. No luck. She put the last of their saltine crackers in his food bowl and found him dead the next morning. She briefly considered making Roberto into a broth, then rejected the idea and put him in the building's dumpster. She told Tía Conchita she had buried him—a little white lie that wouldn't hurt.

There were violent protests every day. People were being killed in the streets daily. Young people, younger than she was. Fred, from the youth orchestra, had been brutally beaten by the police on his way to a rehearsal. He had been carrying his violin. Genesis had watched the videos of Fred trying to explain that he was a musician on his way to the theatre; he was definitely not participating in the protests. But the police beat him and sent him to jail. Genesis didn't know Fred personally, but many of her colleagues did. No one dared to interfere because they were afraid. Genesis, too, was afraid. Making her way to the theatre for a rehearsal when a protest was planned made her feel like she was trapped in one of those horror movies she used to watch as a teenager. Never could she have imagined that in her country it would become possible for a musician to be beaten up for walking down the wrong street with their violin. As if a violin were a weapon. Armando, the violist, was killed by a bullet during another protest. He had just been accepted into medical school. Willy Arteaga's violin had been destroyed by a member of the national guard during another protest, and even though the video of his abuse had gone viral, he was still arrested and tortured, and beaten so savagely that he lost his hearing in one ear. He said he had watched the guards rape a girl right next to him. Genesis knew full well that while men were brutally treated, women always had it worse. She was no exception. They were all trapped. Born to be prey. And Licenciado Héctor López Méndez thought the situation was hard for him?

"Yes, I understand that, Licenciado." Genesis felt queasy but forced herself to stay calm. She needed that passport. She needed to make it to her audition in Toronto. She needed to leave Caracas. "I brought something that I thought perhaps you might accept as a token of my appreciation and gratitude." Hoping for the best, she put her hand into her blouse to free the gold chain and treble-clef charm. She placed it on the desk for Licenciado López Méndez to see. He picked it up with his Bratwurst fingers and examined it. "Eighteen-karat gold," she added, feigning enthusiasm. "They don't use that anymore."

Licenciado López Méndez looked pleased. He opened his top drawer and put the chain inside. "I'll accept this as a demonstration of your good faith," he said. Genesis let out a sigh of relief. "But it will only grant you a discount."

"A discount?" She should have known. How could she have been so stupid? But there was no stopping now. "How much more will it be?"

"Señorita Genesis, I want to help you. You will need your savings for your trip. Didn't you just say so?"

The sound of a siren from the street below pierced the air. Genesis wished someone were coming to her aid. She remembered the siren on the day that Tía Conchita had died. Her dear old aunt had been unable to eat for several days, she had refused all water, and her body was a constellation of bed sores that Genesis had no means of treating. The paramedics had removed Tía Conchita's body—the shell that used to contain that beautiful woman's mind and spirit—on a stretcher while Genesis stood crying by the door. "Died of natural causes," said the certificate. Genesis had shaken her head. Natural causes. Yes, it was only natural for people to die under these circumstances.

Licenciado López Méndez stood up and stretched his arms. Genesis focused on the round sweat stains that had grown under his armpits. He signalled with his chin for her to move to the loveseat behind her while he walked towards the door. He opened it briefly to tell his secretary that this meeting was going to be prolonged, as there were issues in Señorita Genesis's application that he needed to go over. He would have the paperwork ready in an hour so that her passport could be expedited. Genesis thought she should react in some way to this wonderful news. Wasn't this what she had come for? But her body didn't react; she couldn't utter a single word. Her mind had become disconnected from her limbs and her mouth. She was a puppet with broken strings.

"Go have lunch now, there'll be work to do later this afternoon," Licenciado López Méndez told his secretary before closing the door and turning the lock. Genesis's heart began to pound. Was the secretary in on this? Was that why she had barely looked up when Genesis introduced herself earlier? How could she work for this vile man? Genesis felt glued to the pleather chair. Her entire body trembled.

"Well?" Licenciado López Mendez was unbuckling his belt.

Genesis put her hands on the arms of the chair and took a deep breath. She remembered Tía Conchita's last moments. She had been so weak that she could barely fight against the pillow that Genesis held over her face. "Forgive me, Tía Conchita, forgive me. I can't do this anymore," she had whispered, crying. "Forgive me." Despite the pain and the tears, she managed to keep her arms steady until she was sure the breathing had stopped. Then she wailed into that very same pillow and collapsed at the side of the bed. For how long? Who knows? She lost track of time. She was genuinely distraught and disoriented when the police and the paramedics arrived.

Natural causes.

Like this, she thought. She had caused this to happen. She should have known better than to set foot in this office. But now it was too late. It was only natural. Time to pay. Two thousand dollars? Was that what her body and her dignity were worth? All of a sudden it no longer seemed like a fortune. "Forgive me, Tía Conchita," she thought, as she felt Licenciado López Méndez's Bratwurst fingers fondling her breasts from behind the chair. Genesis closed her eyes.

She Who Laughs Last

"BY THE WAY, Rita called."

Veronica turned around abruptly to look at Michael.

"What did she want?"

"To congratulate us."

For a few seconds, they remained silent.

"She invited me to go for a drink, actually. To say goodbye."

Veronica shrugged. She had decided to feign indifference whenever Michael spoke of Rita, but at the mention of her name, Veronica had begun to feel queasy.

"When?" she asked, turning her back to him again.

Twisting the ring Michael had recently given her, Veronica thought about Rita. Her white skin and those dark eyes that had stared intently into hers, first with sweetness and admiration, then later with contempt. She would never forget the day Michael admitted he was having an affair with Rita. That evening at the hospital was as vivid a memory as the scars on her wrists — scars she no longer bothered to cover with the sleeves of her sweater. She could barely recall the physical pain, but the emotional pain she felt when she awoke in the white hospital room, knowing that Michael was no longer with her, was unmistakable. He was with Rita. Michael. And. Rita.

Veronica suddenly felt like getting up, going over to Michael, and threatening him. She wanted to tell him that if he went out with Rita, when he came back she would no longer be here. She felt like removing her ring and throwing it in his face, but instead she squeezed it harder between her hands. She didn't want to fight with Michael over Rita anymore. The only thing that mattered now was that he had come back to her, that he had asked her to forgive him and promised that they'd spend the rest of their lives together. Veronica smiled, telling herself that there was nothing Rita could do now to prevent their happiness. She had won. And Rita knew it. It was clear that she knew it. Rita had always been a sore loser, but this time she'd just have to resign herself to it.

Veronica breathed a sigh of satisfaction. At that moment she felt a compelling urge to go along with Michael on his date, if only to gloat about her triumph. To take him by the hand and show Rita once and for all to whom he really belonged. *To me*, she said to herself. The pride building inside her made Veronica abandon the idea of accompanying Michael. All right, deep down, the prospect of their meeting again did trouble her a bit, but she was determined not to let it show.

"Go ahead," she kissed him. "And make it clear this will be the last time."

THE NEXT DAY, Veronica regretted her decision. When Michael came to say goodbye, she was about to tell him to stay, that she'd changed her mind. But she just caressed his neck, right at the spot where she had left the purplish imprint of her teeth the night before so that Rita would see it. Holding Michael's arm, she walked him to the front door and watched as he disappeared among the cars. She loved to watch him ride his motorcycle.

For the next few hours, Veronica remained seated in front of the television. But after a while she could no longer concentrate on any of the programs. She checked her watch every minute, glancing towards the telephone or the door in the hope of hearing the lock turning. She kept changing the channel, trying not to imagine why Michael was taking longer than she had expected. She tried to focus her attention on the screen, but found it impossible to control the ideas that popped incessantly into her head. For a while she found consolation thinking that he'd probably run into a friend and gone for another drink. *Anybody can lose track of time in a situation like that*, she told herself. Then she began to feel ill. She switched off the TV. She walked back and forth between the kitchen and the window that opened onto the street, taking advantage of each trip to snack on something. She ate an entire box of cookies before deciding to pour herself a shot of tequila, but she could only take one sip. She was thinking of Rita. Of her white skin and elusive eyes, so different and yet so similar to her own. She tried her best not to cry, but at dawn, when sleep began to overtake her and Michael had still not returned, she couldn't hold back the tears.

WHEN VERONICA AWOKE, it was almost noon. She could hardly get out of bed because of a nasty stomach ache. "Fuckin' cookies," she kept mumbling as she packed up Michael's things in a suitcase. She'd decided to throw him out of the house as soon as she saw him through the window. She wasn't even going to let him in. This time, Rita wouldn't be able to enjoy the scene of Veronica being abandoned. This time, she would be the one to take the initiative. Veronica set the suitcase next to the door and sat down beside the window to watch the street. She mentally reviewed the phrases she wanted to scream at Michael.

Carefully chosen insults and curses, the ones she was sure would hurt him the most.

When evening arrived, she started to think that he might have had an accident on the motorcycle, but the idea frightened her so much that she preferred to discard it. Veronica remained attentive until it was almost midnight, looking alternately at her watch, the empty street, and the trash can, full of damp tissues and the coloured-paper wrappers of her favourite chocolates. She gave up several hours later but didn't go to bed without first drinking a much larger dose of laxative than usual. Yes, nearly four dozen chocolates — or more? When did she lose count? She'd eaten too many...

IT WAS DAWN when Veronica arrived at Rita's house. She was expecting to find Michael there. Veronica no longer cared what Rita might say when she saw her. All she cared about was that the two were together again. All she wanted was to insult him, to hit him. To throw his ring on the floor and spit in his face.

"Where's Michael?"

"What's wrong?"

Even though Rita looked surprised, Veronica thought she was lying again, so she went on.

"Either he comes out or —"

"He's not here, Veronica."

She looked at Rita with incredulity.

"I swear it's true. I haven't seen him since the day before yesterday."

Rita was wearing the same perfume she always wore. It distracted Veronica. She wondered how Rita — how Michael — could like such a sweet smell.

"He hasn't come home since he left to see you." Veronica had to make a big effort not to break down. She started biting her nails to control herself.

"That's not my problem. And cover up those arms of yours, Jesus! You look pathetic."

Veronica backed out of the entryway and Rita slammed the door.

Veronica didn't know what to do. She hurried back to the apartment in case Michael had returned. But when she arrived, the suitcase was untouched by the door and there was still no sign of him.

VERONICA SPENT THE next few hours calling her friends, the police, and all the local hospitals. Finally, she called the office where she worked to explain what had happened and let them know that she wouldn't be coming in. At that moment she wasn't worried about her job; all she could think about was Michael. Veronica was feeling increasingly desperate and guilty because she had allowed him to go see Rita alone. She took a photo of Michael and went to the bar where he was supposed to meet Rita, but none of the servers recognized him. When she got back to the apartment, she took Michael's clothes out of the suitcase and put them back in their places more neatly than ever. As she put them in the drawers and the closet, she chided herself for having planned to insult him. She only wanted to see him again, for things to be the way they were the day before. Almost without thinking, she put on Michael's grey sweater; it still had the slight scent of his cologne. She let the sleeves completely cover her fingers. She resolved not to take it off until Michael returned.

The following afternoons and evenings Veronica stayed by the window with the telephone on her lap and her eyes glued to the sidewalk. She hoped at any moment to spot Michael making his way up to the entrance of the building. She didn't feel like eating any more candy or fixing herself a drink. She avoided any task that would take her away from her post. She only went to the kitchen to get water when her thirst was unbearable, when her legs began to ache.

THE CALL WAS brief. Would she please come to the police station to identify Michael's motorcycle? It was only missing a few pieces. But of Michael there was not a trace. Veronica learned that it had been found near the bar where he had planned to meet Rita, so she decided to return there and ask again. This time a young man recognized his photograph.

"I think I saw him leave with a girl."

Veronica hurried off without stopping to ask for details or thank him for the information. She felt the same pain as that morning in the hospital.

"TELL ME WHAT you did to him."

Rita smiled and shook her head. "Poor thing. You look awful. You could have at least put on a clean sweater, you know?"

Veronica stared at her imploringly. Rita's nose looked like a vulture's beak. Veronica shivered.

"What's more, you really need a shower," Rita added.

The sweet smell of her perfume was more aggressive than her eyes.

"Just tell me. Please."

They were quiet for a few seconds. Then Rita looked down at Veronica's hands.

"It looks like that didn't make much of a difference, did it?" she said, nodding at the ring. Then she sighed.

Veronica was going to reply but she couldn't utter a sound. Her eyes were fixed on her ring. Then she noticed her fingers: the raw skin around her cuticles, the dark substance under her nails. Chocolate, dirt, dried blood, or a mix of all three?

Rita watched her in silence and finally let out a nervous giggle. Before slamming the door, she whispered, "Face it, sis. You lost."

Helen's Truth

"I WILL EXPLAIN, gentlemen of the jury..."

I have chosen to begin with the same words my sister uttered during her trial, as we are tied together not only by the curse of blood but by the sharp-edged judgement of both men and gods. Our story is known to all. It has been heard and repeated thousands of times by the thousands of people who envied us before the war and the thousands who have openly condemned us since peace was achieved. My sister was condemned because of her crime; I, because of the affronts that "noble" men, incapable of behaving as anything more than beasts, committed in my name and against my will. Those crimes, however, are not mine. Gentlemen of the jury, you are about to hear the only crime for which I am responsible. You know as well as I do that no woman has ever been the true cause of any war.

My father loathed me from birth because the very moment he saw me he realized I was not his. As you are aware, my mother suffered the same destiny as many women: seduced, taken advantage of, abused. I—as I discovered much later—am the result of that abuse. Do not believe the lies your eyes and ears have fed you. The truth is that for a little girl—even one whose beauty is praised by all—it is hard to cope with rejection from her own father. He was not the one who came to my rescue when Theseus abducted me; that heroic task was performed by my brothers, the twins. And when they arrived it was already too late for me. Too late.

You would have to be torn out of your skin, your flesh exposed and raw, to understand how I felt when that man took me as his prisoner and pulled me away from my home, my city, everything I knew and held dear, and forced me to share his bed. Barely a few moons before had my body delivered in blood the terrible news of my maturity, but I was still a young girl whose only wish was to please her father. Do you have any idea, gentlemen of the jury, how revolted I felt, how much I hated myself when I realized I had been dishonoured? I drowned in shame every time I thought about my family and my people. That is why, once my brothers brought me back home, I told my father—the man I *thought* was my father—that I would do anything to repair his honour. That is how I became a trophy.

Nobody seemed to know — to care — that I had been defiled. The competition to obtain my hand in marriage was a triumph, a legendary event. No one seemed to notice that I spent the entire morning crying. At the end, all I could do was vomit. Yet by contracting nuptials to Menelaus, brother of my sister's husband, I not only tightened our bond — and unknowingly, perhaps too our tragic destinies — but I was blessed with my father's approving smile for the first time in my life. The tears I shed during my wedding did not speak of love for the man who would possess me from that day onwards, but of joy for having earned the approval of the only one for whom I ever cared.

Time passed and my sister gave birth to four children. Yet I — month by cruel month — was cursed by the confirmation of barrenness welling up between my legs. When the foreigner arrived to visit — no, you will not hear me name him; he repulses me so much that I will not pronounce his name — my husband had just spat in my face and called me a sterile creature. My incapacity to have progeny was surely some kind of punishment associated with my origin, he said. That is how I found out what had happened to my mother and how I came to exist.

My entire life I had been struggling for the blessing of a man whose blood was not mine, who had never cared for me. And I had bartered my future to another man for whom, in public, I was a coveted prize, but in private, a disappointment. The foreigner took advantage of my resentment, and when he asked me to elope with him I immediately accepted. I gave not a thought to the consequences.

It is no secret to anyone that my departure unleashed the longest, bloodiest war of our time. I grieve the loss of my niece, and therefore, of my sister, who has vowed never to forgive me. I deeply regret my role, such that it was, in the calamities she was forced to endure and which destroyed her life. But as I said before, no woman has ever been the true cause of any war. Proud men, eager to cleanse with blood the affront of my absconding, dragged countless innocent lives towards their untimely end just to satisfy their vanity. I will never feel sorry for that. What I will be forever sorry for — no, sorry is too insignificant a word to encompass the incommensurable pain I have hidden for too long — is what I was forced to do when the war was closing in on us. My crime.

The foreigner and I had been living as husband and wife for only a few months when I realized I was with child. I had never felt such a rush of joy. I ran to reveal the news to him, the father-to-be, but instead of sharing my happiness he became enraged. My body, he said, would grow big and unattractive; my skin would lose firmness; war was the worst moment to have a child. He locked me in a room out of his sight until the baby was born. For over two hundred nights I was alone there, living in fear, wondering what would become of me and our future son. But instead of a son, after many hours of agony I gave birth to a daughter. Her father came to see us and was pleased to learn our baby was a girl and that she looked like me.

"Her beauty," he said, "will be of use. Offering her as a gift will create alliances. She will be the solution to this war."

When he left the room, I looked at that little girl—the most beautiful and perfect baby girl ever born, *my* girl— and asked her not to worry. I whispered to her how much I loved her and promised I would always do so. It dawned on me that the same curse that had haunted my life would also be her shadow, but how could I find the words to explain this to her? I offered her my breast and, as I pressed her against me, I knew for a certainty that this was for her benefit, that this would save her from a life of despair and rejection. And so I pressed her against my chest and held her tight, then tighter still, until she stopped moving.

This was not the story you were hoping to hear, gentlemen of the jury. You can see past my beauty now; perhaps now you will cease to understand the world solely by what your eyes tell you. Why commit this unspeakable crime? you must be wondering. It is simple: I could not let my daughter carry the weight of my lineage.

Not a single night has gone by without my yearning for her. Not a single day goes by without my finding relief in her absence. I deserve the harshest of punishments. My sole consolation is knowing for certain that I saved her from the hands and the choices made by men, starting with those of her own father. I saved her from sharing the destiny of her aunt—my beloved Clytemnestra, for whom I beg you to grant compassion—and my own destiny as the most beautiful and wretched woman in the world.

Acknowledgements

NEVER IN MY wildest dreams would I have dared imagine, when I arrived in Canada back in 2003, that one day my work would be published by the prestigious House of Anansi Press. I still feel I need someone to pinch me!

They say it takes a village to raise a child but, in my experience, it is also true that it takes a village to help a writer craft a book, work through its many drafts, and have it published. This short story collection would not exist had I not received the amount of support I was fortunate, and humbled, to receive.

Thank you, Verónica Flores, for believing in me, and for being the best literary agent anyone could dream of. Without your hard work and insight, my manuscript would never have made it this far. Everyone at VF Agencia Literaria in Mexico City has been amazing throughout this process, particularly Ana Karen Larios, who is in charge of foreign rights and helped me travel the path here. *Gracias, gracias, gracias a todas ustedes.*

Thank you, Janie Yoon, for opening this amazing door for my stories. Mariana Linares also deserves a big shout-out for spotting my manuscript and thinking it would be a good fit for this wonderful publishing house, *qué suerte la mía, gracias de verdad.* Janie, I will always cherish our Zoom meeting right at the beginning of this adventure and will be forever in your debt for your generous comments and trust in my writing.

And of course, a ginormous thank you to Douglas Richmond, who oversaw the completion of this book and whose careful and clever edits taught me so very much and helped me polish each one of these stories. I appreciate your patience, Doug, and how respectfully and thoroughly you revised my work. You welcomed your baby daughter while we were working on my manuscript, and in spite of how busy new parents are (and have every right to be), you were always there to answer my long emails full of questions and requests. I felt truly accompanied (and heard!) by you, from beginning to end. I have no way to repay you for your generosity. Thank you, thank you, thank you. It has been a total pleasure to work with you.

Gracias to everyone at House of Anansi Press for their work to bring this book to life! From the sales to the design department and everywhere in between, I could not be more grateful. Thanks in particular to Karen Brochu, Debby de Groot, Laura Chapnick, Jessey Glibbery, Alysia Shewchuk, Laura Brady, Joshua Greenspon, Allegra Robinson, and the rest of the team. It's such an honour to count on your talent and knowledge. Kate Juniper Vandergugten, thanks for your attention to detail and for your wonderful letter, which I will forever treasure. Lucia Kim, your cover and interior design are stunning. I am in awe of your creativity and talent. Thanks for giving my stories such a gorgeous face! Grace Shaw, your wisdom and meticulousness saved me: thanks for your patience and kindness. Thanks also to all the talented writers who agreed to read my book and offer their support.

As an immigrant to Canada and a writer striving to have a career in a language other than my own, I have been very privileged to count on the continuous support and big-heartedness of Barry Callaghan and everyone at Exile Editions, who were the first to publish my work in English. I will forever be grateful to Barry, Michael, and Nina Callaghan, as well as to my gorgeous amiga Gabriela Campos, for opening the door for me as a writer and a friend. Gracias, Exile!

Here in Canada, I am very fortunate to work with a group of Latino/Hispanic-Canadian writers called Imagina. Together, we have had the pleasure of curating two very successful anthologies, *Historias de Toronto* and *Historias de Montreal*, through which I have met many wonderful and talented people. I want to thank my dear José Antonio Villalobos and Juan Gavasa, and Dr. Ingrid Bejerman, for their invaluable friendship and support.

The stories in this book went through several revisions before being submitted for House of Anansi's consideration. Thankfully, a group of talented and generous women, all of them in love with the nuances and the cadence of the English language, generously lent me their eyes and wisdom to tweak them.

At the top of this girl-power list is my Fairy Godmother, Dr. Gillian Bartlett. I have learned so much from you, dearest FG! Thank you for always being there for me, thank you for your patience, generosity, and love, and thank you for waving your magic wand over my writing (and my brain!). Without your support (and Ken's), I wouldn't be here.

Amy Stuart, writer and mentor extraordinaire: thank you for your perceptiveness, for your incredibly useful feedback, and for cheering me on.

Jan (and Don) Cross, thanks to you, "Bear Hug" came to be. Thank you for everything you have done for me (us!) throughout the years, for your company, your love and kindness, and for sharing this very intimate family story.

Debra Bennett, thanks for agreeing to read my stories (even though I know they upset you). Your comments are always on point! Thanks as well for introducing me to the Griffin Poetry Prize Readings, where together we listened to the great Ko Un.

Miriam López-Villegas, the most adventurous and self-less woman I have ever met, thanks for always finding time to read and give me valuable feedback for my work, no matter which time zone you are in, or how much humani-tarian work you need to do!

Katy Alchoufi and Corallys Cordero, *un millón de gracias* for helping me make sure "The Audition" was true to the tragic suffering of the Venezuelan people. My solidarity with your homeland, which used to be mine, too. May we all see it free and thriving again soon. Katy, *gracias también por prestarme a Roberto.*

Mariana Roca, my partner-in-crime for everything having to do with writing and editing and more: thanks for your clever input and for your friendship.

Finding the strength and encouragement to write even during the darkest or busiest moments in life is not easy, especially when, more often than not, it can feel like all your efforts are leading nowhere. I have been very lucky to count on wonderful people—be it friends, colleagues, or writers I admire—to push me forward so I could reach my goals.

Julia Edler, my lifelong friend, danke schön for always championing my literary work.

Marina Nemat, what a terrific example you have set for me and for countless other people. Thank you for your friendship, and for helping me believe this was possible.

Pura López-Colomé, *gracias por existir*. You are always a source of inspiration. Thanks for your faith in me.

Rosemary Sullivan, counting on your friendship and support is an honour. Thanks for your kindness!

Lawrence Hill, thank you so much for your endorsement of my work. I will never forget your generosity, kindness, and warmth.

Tina Kilbourne, thanks for your enduring friendship and solidarity since those early Muskoka Novel Marathon Days. I'm very grateful for your support.

Herejes y Chingonatas, escribir y maternar en tribu con ustedes es lo máximo. Gracias.

Banda de la Schule, you know who you are, and you also know how important you are to me. *Danke sehr* for all these decades of love, friendship, and fun. Mana Patipi-tipi y Nenas, *ailoviu mucho.*

Sadly, none of my first mentors are alive to see this book. I want to take this opportunity, however, to pay a little homage to them. Their wisdom shaped my thoughts and writing, as well as my own teaching method, and I know that wherever they may be now, they are celebrating these stories with me. Thanks, beloved Uncle Huberto Batis, and thank you, Daniel Sada, Alí Chumacero, Carlos

Montemayor, Sandro Cohen, and René Avilés Fabila, for sharing your knowledge with me as I took my initial steps down this path.

My mother, concert pianist Eva María Zuk, passed away on February 27, 2017, at just seventy-one years old. I know she would have loved to see this book. "The First Piano" was inspired by a concert she gave in a tiny town in the state of Hidalgo, Mexico, when I was a little girl. People actually did carry their best chairs into the church where she played the first classical music recital they ever attended. Both my mother and my father, retired orchestra conductor Enrique Bátiz (who, at the time this book is released, will be turning eighty years young: happy birthday, Papito querido!), worked tirelessly to share the joy and beauty of classical music on all possible stages in Mexico, Latin America, and the world. I want to thank them for raising me in a home filled with music, which has had such great influence on my writing, and for giving me an amazing little brother I'm glad not to have accidentally killed when we were children. Tito, *te quiero muchísimo.* Thanks for always being there.

And last, but never least, I need to thank my incredibly supportive husband, Dr. Edgar Tovilla. Thank you for holding the fort for me when I need to take time off to write, thanks for believing in me, and for the twenty-two years we've spent together, growing both as a couple and as individuals, finding our footing as professionals in Canada, our home and adoptive land, and raising our three adorable children. Ivana, Natalia, Marco: thanks for your patience when Mom needs to write. I'm incredibly proud of you and love you more than words can say.

Credit: Emily Ding

MARTHA BÁTIZ is an award-winning writer, translator, and professor of Spanish language and literature. She is the author of six books, including the story collection *Plaza Requiem*, winner of an International Latino Book Award, and the novella *Boca de lobo* (translated from the Spanish as *Damiana's Reprieve*), winner of the Casa de Teatro Prize. Born and raised in Mexico City, Martha Bátiz lives in Toronto.

www.marthabatiz.com